Michael Bond

The Great Big Paddington Book

GALLERY BOOKS
An Imprint of W. H. Smith Publishers Inc.
112 Madison Avenue
New York City 10016

ISBN 0 8317 4007 8

First published in 5 volumes by William
Collins Sons & Co Ltd as:
The Great Big Paddington Book
© Text Michael Bond 1976
© Illustrations Collins 1976

Fun and Games with Paddington
© Text Michael Bond 1977
© Illustrations Collins 1977

Paddington's Party Book
© Text Michael Bond 1976
© Illustrations William Collins Son & Co Ltd 1976

Paddington's Loose-End Book
© Text Michael Bond 1976
© Illustrations William Collins Son & Co Ltd 1976

Paddington's Cartoon Book
© Text Michael Bond 1979
© Illustrations Ivor Wood 1979

Printed and bound in Great Britain by
PURNELL BOOK PRODUCTION LIMITED
A MEMBER OF BPCC plc.

Insides and Cover Design by the Pinpoint Design Company.

32 Windsor Gardens
Lundun.

Dear all.
This is a book for all those who like kartoons, marmalade, making things out of skraps, reading foyrtunes in the bottom of tea-cups, and

← I'm afraid I made
a bit of a mess there when I tried to read my fortune in the bottom of a cocoa-mug, so there is only reelly room to say I hope you enjoy the fun and games in this book as much as I did when I tested them.

Yores Sinseerely
Padingtun

P.S. Mrs Bird says (Don't forget to cleer up any mess you may make afterwords — otherwyse you won't be very poppular (neither will I!)

Contents

Paddington's World Conjuring Tricks

PASSING A BEAR THROUGH A POSTCARD

This trick has always been very popular at the Home for Retired Bears in Lima, and it was passed on to Paddington before he left for England.

If you hold a postcard up in front of your audience and say you will cut a hole in it large enough for someone to crawl through, it sounds impossible. The trick is in the way you cut the hole.

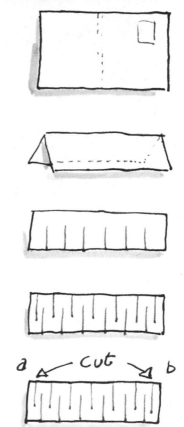

First, fold the postcard in half lengthways as shown.

Next, take a pair of sharp scissors and make a series of cuts from the outer edge inwards, stopping short of the fold.

Follow this with a second series of cuts between the first row, starting from the folded edge and stopping short of the outer edge.

Finally, cut along the folded edge from point (a) to point (b), leaving the two outer folds intact.

The 'postcard' will now open out into a giant ring.

PADDINGTON'S MAGIC CONE

Everyone knows that Paddington has a secret compartment in his suitcase – although very few people know what's inside, and no one but Paddington knows how to open it!

Here's how to make a CONE with a SECRET COMPARTMENT.

You need: a sheet of fairly thin paper twice as long as it is wide (some typing paper 12 inches by 6 inches would be fine).
Now: Lay the paper lengthways on a table in front of you.

1. Fold the right hand edge over to the left, press down on the fold to make a sharp crease, then open it up again.
2. Fold the bottom right hand corner (a) up to point (b), and the top left corner (c) down to point (d). Again, press down firmly on the folds.
3. Fold corner (c) up to point (f). Press flat.
4. Fold corner (g) down to (h), press flat and open up again.
5. Holding the same corner (g), tuck it inside the fold (h-i), pushing it right inside until you have made a flat triangular shape.

You will find that by holding the triangle with one hand at either point (x) or point (y) you can make a cone by poking a finger of your other hand into the fold on the opposite side.

To make small, flat objects disappear, ask a member of your audience to drop, say, a small coin inside it.

Then, by sleight of paw, or by placing it under a cloth while you distract their attention, you simply turn the paper cone over, hold the opposite corner and open up the second cone. Presto! The object will have disappeared!

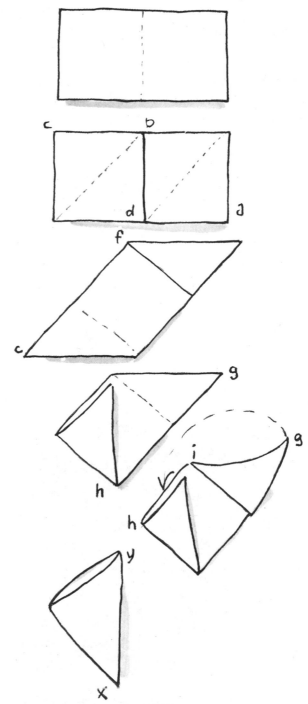

To make this trick look even more professional the cone can be painted, but if it is, make sure the pattern is the same on either side, otherwise the audience will see you have reversed it.

How to make a 'Secret Compartment'

If you ask most magicians to name their favorite color, the chances are they will say BLACK. And the duller the black, that is to say the less shiny it is, the better – because then it won't reflect the light or show up unwanted shadows.

This is why most magicians tend to wear evening dress or dark suits, and perform their tricks against black backgrounds.

You can take advantage of this very useful fact if you wish to make yourself a secret compartment.

Paddington has a secret compartment in his suitcase, which he uses to keep his important papers in. No one, apart from Paddington himself, has ever seen inside it, but if you would like one too here's how it can be done using an old shoe box and a few other bits and pieces.

You will need:

   1. **A cardboard shoe box.**

   2. **Enough decorative self adhesive paper to cover the outside.**

   3. **A piece of fairly heavy cardboard slightly larger than the box.**

   4. **Two strips of thinner card about 2 inches wide and slighly less in length than the width of the box.**

   5. **Matt black paint.**

   6. **Glue.**

How to make it:

1. Remove the lid from the box and cover the whole of the outside of both lid and box with the decorative paper.

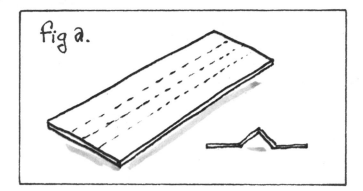

fig a.

2. Measure the width and length of the *inside* of the box and carefully cut the sheet of cardboard to fit. (It should be as exact as possible – not too loose, and certainly not too tight.)

3. Draw three lines half an inch apart along the length of the cardboard strips, score with a knife and fold as shown in fig a.

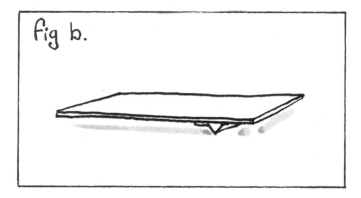

fig b.

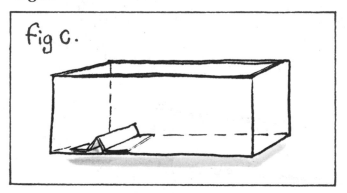

fig c.

4. Glue one of these strips to the underneath side of the false bottom as in fig b.

5. Glue the second strip across the inside of the bottom of the box as in fig c.

6. Paint the whole of the inside of the box and the lid black, then paint both sides of the false bottom.
Allow to dry.

7. Drop the false bottom into place. Slide pressure at either end will cause the opposite end to rise up.

If you have cut out the cardboard neatly it will be very hard to detect the false bottom. You can of course make a more sophisticated version using, say, an old cigar box, thin plywood, and strips of balsa wood; but the same principles apply.

Paddington Takes the Biscuit

Glancing up from the book he was reading, Paddington directed a hard stare in the direction of his bedroom wall, and then pulled his hat firmly down over his ears.

He didn't often wear his hat indoors – he was much too well brought up for that; but for once he had a number of very good reasons for the lapse, all of which were taking place at that very moment on the other side of the wall.

Mrs. Brown and her housekeeper, Mrs. Bird, were clearing out the guest room, and if the noise was anything to go by they were having a field day; vacuuming, emptying drawers, turning the mattress, and generally sorting through all the odds and ends and pieces of junk which had accumulated since the room had last been used.

That morning they had received unexpected news that their niece, Juliet, was arriving from France. What made matters worse was the fact that the letter had been delayed in the mail, and far from their niece giving them the week's notice she had obviously intended, she was due to arrive that very afternoon.

Paddington had never actually met Juliet, but as soon as he heard that she was coming he got out an old phrase book so that he could surprise everyone by welcoming her in her second language.

The book listed several different ways of saying 'hello' in French, some of which – if the number of words was anything to go by – seemed very good value indeed; but there was so much noise going on in the next room he could hardly remember a simple greeting like *Bonjour*, let alone anything more complicated.

He had several tries at *comment allez-vous?*, but then gave it up in disgust. Even if he had been able to ask the Browns' niece how she was, he certainly wouldn't have been able to understand her if she told him.

He was about to have one last try when Mrs. Brown's voice came floating through the open window again. "I should throw those pillows down on the lawn," she called to Mrs. Bird. "They've gone quite lumpy with age. I'll give them a going over later."

Her words were the signal for some more ructions. Either Mrs. Bird's aim hadn't been up to scratch, or she didn't know her own strength, for it seemed the pillows had sailed clean over the Browns' fence and landed slap bang in the middle of the lawn belonging to their next door neighbour, Mr. Curry.

Paddington heaved a sigh. It was obviously one of 'those days', and clearly he wasn't going to learn much French that morning. In fact his head was in such a whirl he didn't know whether he was *vennezing* or *allezing*, so he put down his book and hurried into the next room in order to lend a helping paw. The sooner the job was done the better it would be for all concerned.

"Really!" exclaimed Mrs. Brown, as he entered the room. "That man takes the biscuit!"

"Mr. Curry's taken our biscuits!" exclaimed Paddington in alarm. He hurried across to join the others at the window and was just in time to see the Browns' neighbour disappear into his kitchen, slamming the door behind him.

"I hope they weren't some of my special coconut ones," he added hotly. Mr. Curry had a reputation for meanness, but even he had never sunk that low before.

"It's not your biscuits I'm worried about." said Mrs. Bird crossly. "It's our pillows. He's

taken them!" She picked up a pile of blankets and headed towards the door. "I've enough to do without things like that happening."

"Oh, dear," said Mrs. Brown. She looked around for some way of occupying Paddington, and as she did so her eyes alighted on a small china figure.

"Perhaps you could find a home for that?" she suggested. "I don't want it to get broken."

Paddington didn't need to be asked twice. What with the loss of his biscuits and the

pillows into the bargain, things were getting a bit too complicated for his liking, and after putting on his duffle coat he set off and was soon hurrying down Windsor Gardens in the direction of the market.

It was a bright Spring morning, and having called in at the baker's for his morning supply of buns, he turned a corner into Portobello Road and headed towards the antique shop belonging to his friend, Mr. Gruber.

Mr. Gruber was standing on the sidewalk taking in the morning sunshine, and as Paddington drew near he held out his hand. "Don't tell me you're setting up in business too, Mr. Brown," he said, catching sight of the china figure in Paddington's paw.

"Oh, no, Mr. Gruber," said Paddington. "I'm looking for a home for it. That's why I came to see you."

Mr. Gruber took the object from Paddington and turned it upside down in order to examine it more closely. "If I'm not mistaken," he said excitedly, "this is a piece of genuine Sèvres porcelain. It's from the French biscuit period."

"The French *biscuit* period?" exclaimed Paddington in surprise as he followed Mr. Gruber into the shop. "It's a good job Mr. Curry didn't get hold of it."

While Mr. Gruber busied himself making some cocoa for their morning break the back of the shop, Paddington related the morning's events.

"Perhaps I can help," said Mr. Gruber, as he settled himself down on the Chesterfield beside Paddington. "I could put it in my window for the time being and see what happens. It's probably one of a pair, and if the other one ever turns up it might be quite valuable. The world of art is much smaller than you might think, Mr. Brown. Word soon gets around and you never know your luck."

Mr. Gruber stood up and placed the figure reverently between a small Toby jug and a brass plant pot in his window, and then turned the conversation back to the Browns' niece.

"I shall look forward to meeting her," he said dreamily. "It'll take me back to when I was a young student living in Paris. I used to spend most of my time wandering around the Flea markets in those days."

Paddington was so surprised at this piece of information he nearly dropped his bun in the cocoa by mistake. The thought of Mr. Gruber going to a market in search of fleas made him feel quite itchy.

Mr. Gruber gave a chuckle as he caught sight of the expression on Paddington's face.

"They don't have *real* fleas there, Mr. Brown," he said. "At least, not for sale; although you may pick up one or two by accident." And he went on to explain that the Paris markets were not unlike the one on Portobello Road, except that most of them were older and dealt more in junk than in genuine antiques.

"But it's possible to pick up some very good bargains there," he continued. "In fact, that's where I first became interested in the business."

Mr. Gruber pointed to the china figure. "For all we know that may have spent some of its days there. I wouldn't mind betting it could tell quite a story if it liked."

Mr. Gruber looked as if he could have chatted for the rest of that day as well, but interesting though he was, Paddington had to get back to Windsor Avenue, so a moment or two later he said goodbye and left.

When he reached home Paddington found that quite a lot had been happening while he'd been away. The spare room was all ready; the rest of the family were all busy changing; and in the kitchen he found a cake Mrs. Bird had made especially for the occasion. The pink frosting still had a wet shine to it, and she had even written the word JULIET across the top in white.

It was the sight of Mrs. Bird's half-full

frosting pipe that gave Paddington an idea. He was still rather unsure of his 'phrases' and he decided the best way of getting them right would be to draw a welcome in French on the actual cake.

After carefully making sure no one was around, he picked up the frosting pipe and gave it a squeeze.

He'd often watched Mrs. Bird frosting her cakes, and she always made it seem very easy, but in the event it turned out to be much harder than it looked.

To start with he squeezed the canvas bag in the wrong place, so that instead of the frosting coming out through the nozzle, a large glob shot out and landed on the floor.

But it was when he tried to squeeze the frosting back into the tube that he really began to get into a mess. It wasn't so much that he couldn't find a spoon large enough to scoop it off the floor; it was more the fact that he stepped in it by mistake and slipped, putting his other paw straight through the top of the cake.

Paddington pressed the cake back together as best he could and then eyed it gloomily. He'd only been inside the kitchen a few minutes and yet already a great change had come over it. As for the writing on the cake, the word JULIET was barely recognisable, and his own letters had turned out so large he hardly had room for the BON, let alone a JOUR to follow.

At that moment the door bell rang, and after giving the cake a final smooth with his paw, he hurried out of the kitchen and joined in the general rush to the front door.

The Browns' niece wasn't at all as he had imagined. He'd half expected to see someone wearing a beret and carrying a string of onions over her shoulder, whereas she turned out to be tall and slim, with long fair hair, and a smile which made him feel immediately at ease.

"How do you do?" she said, bending down so that Paddington could kiss her cheeks in true French style. "I've heard so much about you."

Paddington wiped his mouth carefully with the back of his paw, and then did as he was bidden.

"I'm sorry about the frosting," he said, peering up at Juliet's face. "It was supposed to say 'Bonjour', but I'm afraid I had a bit of an accident with the 'jour' when it fell on the floor."

If the Browns' niece was surprised by this piece of information she managed to conceal it very well; although shortly afterwards she disappeared up to her room saying she felt tired after her long journey and wanted to tidy up. She was gone some time, and when she did return it was noticeable that she gave Paddington a very wide berth indeed.

"I hope you don't mind my asking," she said to Mrs. Brown during dinner, "but I've been looking for that china figure I passed on to you. Not that it matters, of course," she added quickly. "It's all rather silly really, but when I

sent it to you I felt I would never want to see it again, and now . . . just lately . . ."

She broke off as a choking sound came from Paddington's direction. "Is anything the matter?"

"Er . . . yes . . . and no," said Paddington truthfully. "I think perhaps something went down the wrong way by mistake." And before any more questions could be asked he hastily filled his fork with a generous helping of everything in sight and opened his mouth in order to down it.

He'd caught Mrs. Brown's eye, and the message was all too clear; she had obviously forgotten all about the ornament until that moment, and now she wanted it back again with all possible speed.

Paddington was up bright and early the next morning, and long before the rest of the family came downstairs he was heading towards the market and Mr. Gruber's shop.

"Oh, no!" said Mr. Gruber, when he heard the reason for Paddington's early appearance. "I'm afraid I have some bad news for you, Mr.

Brown. That ornament has been sold. Not long after you left yesterday someone came past and bought it on the spot. It was a Mr. Fitzgerald and he gave me a very good price for it indeed."

Rummaging inside his desk, Mr. Gruber produced a small notebook. "There's only one hope. He left the address where he's staying. It's not far from here. Perhaps if you go along to see him and explain what's happened he'll let you have it back. You can only try."

Paddington thanked Mr. Gruber for his trouble, and hurried on his way. Three bus stops and some time later he arrived outside a small white house in a rather fashionable street, and rang the bell. There was a pause and then the door opened to reveal a young man wearing pyjamas and dressing gown.

Mr. Fitzgerald looked as if he hadn't been awake for long either, but as he listened to Paddington's tale of woe his sleepy expression disappeared as if by magic.

"This is too much to hope for!" he exclaimed,

holding the door open for Paddington to enter. "You'd better come inside. I'd like to hear the whole story all over again." And he led the way into the dining room, where a table was set for breakfast.

Paddington's eyes glistened as he caught sight of the spread laid out before him. All the rushing around was making him feel very hungry. "I expect I could tell you as many times as you like, Mr. Fitzgerald," he announced eagerly, spotting the marmalade.

"This lady's name," broke in Mr. Fitzgerald urgently. "You're sure it's Juliet . . . from France?"

"Oh, yes," said Paddington. "I put my paw through her cake only yesterday."

"Stay here while I change!" commanded Mr. Fitzgerald. "Help yourself. Dig into the marmalade. There's plenty more where that came from. Only don't go away. I'll only be a moment or two. Whatever you do, don't go away."

"I won't," said Paddington happily, as he stretched out a paw for the marmalade. He had no intention whatsoever of going away before he had to, but unfortunately Mr. Fitzgerald was as good as his word and he barely had time to

open the jar before his host returned, fully dressed and ready to leave.

Mr. Fitzgerald could hardly contain himself. All the way back to number thirty-two Windsor Gardens he kept tapping on the taxi driver's shoulder, calling on him to hurry, and as they climbed the steps of the Browns' house his excitement was so great he almost dropped a small cardboard box he was carrying.

As luck would have it, the Browns' niece herself answered the door. She stood stock still for a moment or two, her hand to her mouth, hardly able to believe her eyes.

"Hamish!" she cried at last.

"Juliet!" exclaimed Mr. Fitzgerald.

"Excuse me!" said Paddington.

Removing his hat, he was just in time to catch Mr. Fitzgerald's box as it fell unheeded from his grasp.

But he had yet another surprise in store, for as he caught it the lid fell open revealing two small white objects, one of which was very familiar indeed.

"My ornament!" gasped Juliet, as she caught sight of it.

"*Our* ornament," corrected Mr. Fitzgerald gently.

"Mercy me!" exclaimed Mrs. Bird, as she and Mrs. Brown appeared at the kitchen door. "Don't say you two know each other."

"Know each other?" Juliet and Mr. Fitzgerald exchanged glances. "We were going to get married!"

"You see," said Juliet, turning to Paddington, "we bought those two china figures when we got engaged."

"In Paris," broke in Mr. Fitzgerald. "In the Flea Market. And when we . . . er, that is *I* . . . broke it off . . . I kept mine."

The Browns' niece lowered her eyes. "And I gave mine away in a fit of pique. One of the reasons I came to stay was that I was hoping to get it back. You can imagine how I felt when I discovered it had gone."

"Just think how I felt when I saw it in a shop window," said Mr. Fitzgerald. "I came to England to forget, and one of the first things I saw was 'our' ornament."

"More to the point," said Mrs. Bird anxiously, "is what is that young bear up to?" She pointed towards Paddington, who was suddenly behaving very strangely indeed; sniffing the china ornaments and licking his lips almost as if he was about to eat them.

"Mr. Gruber said they were biscuits," he announced. "But they seem to have gone very hard."

Mr. Fitzgerald laughed. "He didn't mean they were *real* biscuits," he explained. "I think you might find them rather indigestible. It's just a way of describing very thin porcelain."

"Perhaps I'd better take them," said Juliet. "Otherwise they may get broken."

"I have a much better idea," said Mr. Fitzgerald. "Let's give them both to Paddington. After all," he continued, taking a firm grip of Juliet's arm, "better some broken biscuits in the paw than a broken engagement in France. If he hadn't taken your china figure down to Portobello Road we might never have met each other again. It's a good omen for the future."

"And talking of the future . . . there's a large half-eaten jar of marmalade still on my dining-room table. How about us all going back there for a celebration breakfast?"

"I think," said Paddington, eager to use his French at long last, "that's a very *bon* idea indeed, Mr. Fitzgerald. I've never been to a celebration breakfast before, and biscuits make you hungry – especially when you can't eat them."

Paddington's Christmas Problem

One of the things Paddington liked most about visiting his friend Mr. Gruber on Portobello Road, was the fact that he knew, if he had any sort of problem at all, Mr. Gruber wouldn't dream of letting him go on his way before he'd found the answer.

Which was why, one winter's morning just before Christmas, found Paddington sitting on the Chesterfield at the back of Mr. Gruber's shop, stirring a cup of hot cocoa, and chatting about the subject of presents.

With five members of the Brown family to buy for, he'd run out of ideas long ago; and with everything so expensive he'd almost run out of his 'bun reserves money' as well.

Mr. Gruber looked at him thoughtfully. "Have you ever thought of making your own presents, Mr. Brown?" he asked.

"It's a bit difficult with paws, Mr. Gruber," said Paddington doubtfully.

"Nonsense!" exclaimed Mr. Gruber. "It's all a matter of confidence. Plus a few bits and pieces, of course . . . but I'm sure we can put our hands on plenty of those. And they'll be much more valuable if you've made them yourself."

Reaching up to a nearby shelf, he took down a pile of books, and in no time at all he'd written out a list of things Paddington could make.

"Ladies first," he said, and he began by showing Paddington how he could make a necklace for Judy.

JUDY'S NECKLACE

Materials: old magazines, strong thread or fishing line, scissors, strong glue, pencil, ruler, clear varnish, paintbrush.

What to do:
Cut a piece of thread or fishing line long enough to make a necklace that will slip easily over the wearer's head. Look for colorful pictures in the magazines – pick lots of varied ones, including some with print on. With the pencil and ruler draw long, narrow triangles at least 6 inches long on the pictures. (The base of the triangles should be as long as you want each bead to be.) Cut them out. Put a line of glue along the foot of the triangle on the wrong side of the illustration and put the thread or fishing line on top.

Now carefully roll up the triangle tightly. When you get towards the tip, apply some more glue and finish rolling, sticking down the end very carefully. Shape the roll with your fingers to get a good round shape. Make enough beads to cover the whole length of the necklace.

When the necklace is finished and all the glue dry, you can paint the beads with clear varnish to make them hard and shiny. If you like, you can insert a small, plain bead – or painted, a short piece of macaroni – between each paper bead for variety.

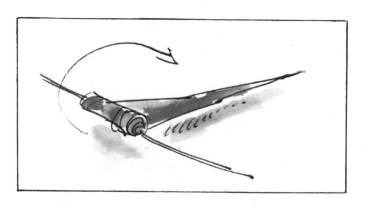

Then came:

Mrs. Brown's Sea-Shell Mirror

Materials: a mirror with a wooden frame (an old one is ideal), small shells, strong glue.

What to do:
Arrange the shells in a pattern on the wooden frame – put any larger ones in a cluster at the top of the frame. Decide where you are going to put everything before you apply any glue. Now take the shells off and spread the glue on the frame – if it is quick drying, do this a patch at a time. Place the shells on the frame in the pattern you had chosen. It is best if the whole frame is covered, with no wood showing through at all.

"You can also decorate picture frames or small boxes in this way," explained Mr. Gruber.

Next, he showed Paddington how to make a POMANDER for Mrs. Bird.

Mrs. Bird's Pomander

Materials: 1 orange, quite a lot of cloves, a length of ribbon, pins.

What to do: Tie the ribbon in a crosswise way around the orange, leaving two ends at the top. Secure at the bottom with a pin. Now cover the whole of the orange with cloves – they should be as close together as possible. Tie the ends of ribbon left at the top into a loop.

"The orange and the cloves together make a beautiful scent," Mr. Gruber explained, "and Mrs. Bird can hang it in her clothes closet."

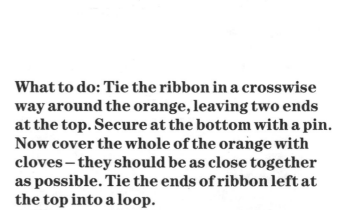

"Even if it doesn't snow," he continued, "I expect there will be some windy days. Why not make Jonathan a CHRISTMAS KITE?"

Jonathan's Kite

Materials: large sheet of plain white paper, pencil, paints, pins, glue, scotchtape, scissors, wire, large ball of string.

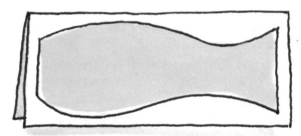

What to do:
Fold the sheet of paper in half lengthwise. Draw a fish shape like this about 30 inches long and 10 inches wide. Paint the shape in a bright, pale color like yellow. When the paint is dry, write on it in large letters the name of the person the kite is for. (Paddington wrote JONATHAN.) Now fill in the letters with bright paint (red is a good choice). When the paint is dry, pin both sides of the paper together and carefully cut out the shape. Unpin and paint a bright design or a message on the other side. (Paddington managed to write 'Merry Christmas' in smaller letters.) When dry, put glue along the top and bottom edges, as shown. But leave each narrow end open.

wire ring

Press the shapes together. Make a ring out of wire like this. Fix it inside the front end with sellotape. The wind can blow through the fish from front to back. So that it can be pulled along, tie a piece of string to each side of the ring and join the ends to a longer piece. If you want to 'fly' the fish really high, it can always be joined in tandem to a more conventional kite.
    Lastly,

Mr. Brown's Tidy Tin
Materials: 1 tin (small cocoa-size, or a large 'economy' size), strong glue, thick string or twine, varnish, paintbrush, newspapers.

What to do:

A small tin will make a 'pencil holder' or somewhere to keep notes. A larger tin will make a waste-paper can. Remove the label from your tin (it comes off easily if you soak the tin in hot water). Make sure the tin is quite dry. Apply glue all round the outside of the tin. (Stand the tin on some newspaper while you do this and hold it by the inside edge.) Start at the bottom and wind the string or twine evenly around the tin – all the way up, until there is no tin left showing. Leave until the glue is dry and then paint on varnish to make the string hard and shiny.

Paddington in Print

Paddington pricked up his ears and paused for a moment, a marmalade sandwich halfway to his mouth.

It was tea-time in the Brown household, and he didn't often allow himself to be diverted from the task in hand, but something Mrs. Brown was saying had given him food for thought.

"Really, Henry!" she'd exclaimed, as she entered the room and dumped a large pile of shopping on the table. "The price of things these days! Money doesn't go anywhere at all."

"If you ask me," said Mr. Brown, "we're all going to have to tighten our belts before it gets any better."

Paddington nearly dropped the remains of his sandwich in alarm.

"We're going to have to tighten our belts, Mr. Brown?" he repeated. "But I haven't even got any suspenders!"

"Mentioning no names," said Mrs. Bird sternly, "there are those among us who would have a job getting a belt round their stomachs in the first place, let alone *tighten* one."

Paddington began to look even more upset as the meaning of this last remark sank in, and shortly afterwards, while the others were busy clearing away the remains of the tea things, he disappeared up to his room.

Once there, he closed the door and began examining his figure in the mirror. Even with his duffle coat on he had to admit the truth of Mrs. Bird's remark. Viewed from any angle he'd put on a bit more weight than was good for him. But even more worrying was the fact that he'd never really thought of the amount of money it must cost the Browns to keep him at all, let alone cope with continually rising prices.

Paddington sat on his bed in order to consider the matter. It was some while before he finally came to a decision, but as soon as he had he hurried downstairs again to tell the others.

The Browns had settled down round the television set for the evening and they were most surprised when he burst into the room. Paddington was normally a very polite bear, but he so obviously had something on his mind they turned their attention away from the screen at once to hear what he had to say.

"I think I would like to take a cut in my bun money," he announced. "It'll help with the housekeeping."

Mrs. Brown looked most affected by this latest turn of events. "Good gracious!" she said. "It's a very kind thought, but there are plenty of people in this world I'd like to see go without their buns before you do."

"There's one for a start," agreed Mrs. Bird firmly. She pointed towards the screen, where a portly figure in striped bathing trunks was being interviewed against the background of a tropical island.

"That's Sir Jasper Stone, the property tycoon. He's made his money living off other people all his life, and now he's making even more out of writing his memoirs telling people how he did it!"

As if to confirm Mrs. Bird's remarks, the figure on the screen flicked a cocktail stick over the side of his yacht and patted his ample stomach.

"I can honestly say," he replied, in answer to an unseen interviewer's question, "that I've never put pen to paper in my life. Apart from signing checks that is."

"But why do you think your book is proving so successful?" persisted the interviewer.

"Because the grass is always greener on the other side of the fence," said Sir Jasper confidently. "People don't want to read about their own dull lives. They want something more exciting and that, quite simply, is what I've given them." He tapped his head. "I wanted the best there is so I employed a ghost writer – someone who would write it for me – and I simply dictated my notes, which I keep up here."

Sir Jasper was obviously just getting into his stride and after another drink had been poured he launched into a long tale about his life and what it was like to be a millionaire playboy.

But Paddington was hardly listening. All of a sudden he'd had yet another idea, and after asking to be excused he hurried back upstairs again.

"I do hope he hasn't taken the matter too much to heart," said Mrs. Brown. "It really was very kind of him to make that offer."

"I wouldn't worry," said Mrs. Bird. "After all, it's the thought that counts and probably by the time the next meal comes around he'll have forgotten all about it."

But for once the Browns' housekeeper had sadly misjudged Paddington's capacity for getting to grips with a problem.

At that very moment he was sitting on his bed clutching his scrapbook with a very faraway look in his eyes indeed. It was an old scrapbook which Mr. Gruber had given to him when he'd first arrived at the Browns. Now, it was almost completely full of notes he'd made about his many adventures, and although bound in the best leather, it had become rather worn and battered over the years.

But in his mind's eye it had already taken on a completely different look. He could even see the title on the spine – FROM DARKEST PERU TO LONDON – THE MEMOIRS OF A BEAR – by PADDINGTON BROWN. He might not have the sort of bestseller on his paws that Sir Jasper Stone had, but he was sure there were lots of things of interest if only they could be put down on paper in the right way.

Paddington's scrapbook had quite a few pages to it and it was late before he finally got to bed that night. Even when he did manage to get to sleep, it was only to dream of interviews on the canoe lake at Brightsea and signing sessions in bookstores, with long lines of would-be customers stretching around the store.

In the past Paddington had often found that ideas dreamed up at night seemed much less good in the cold light of day, but for once it felt quite different. As soon as he woke up he had a hurried breakfast and then announced mysteriously that he had to go out on an important mission.

"I do hope that he's all right," said Mrs. Brown nervously as he disappeared from view down Windsor Gardens. "He brushed his duffle coat before he went out and that's most unusual."

"Bears and their secrets are not very easily parted," said Mrs. Bird wisely, "but I'm sure we'll find out all about it soon enough."

All the same, the Browns' housekeeper would have been very surprised had she been able to see where Paddington finally ended up.

LOVEJOY AND FITCH, the publishers Sir Jasper had chosen for his memoirs, was in a very exclusive part of London. In fact, it didn't look like any sort of office he'd ever seen before, more like some kind of mansion.

In the middle of the entrance hall there was a desk with several telephones on it, and it was occupied by a bored looking girl reading a book.

Paddington approached the desk and raised his hat politely. "Excuse me," he announced, "I'd like to see one of your ghosts if I may."

"Are you going to exorcise it?" asked the girl languidly, hardly bothering too look up.

"I don't think so," said Paddington. "I think I'd rather sit down if you don't mind. I've come a long way and my paws are tired. I was really wanting to see one of them about writing my memoirs."

"Your *memoirs*?" The girl's face suddenly cleared. "Oh, you mean you want to see one of our *ghost writers*? Where did you say you were from?"

"Well," said Paddington. "I didn't. But it's Peru. *Darkest* Peru, and . . ."

But he got no further. The girl's face suddenly changed.

"*Peru!* Do forgive me. I had no idea. Our Mr. Fitch is expecting you. Please come this way."

Looking most surprised at this sudden change of tone, Paddington followed the girl down a long, oak-panelled corridor.

Paddington had never been in a publisher's office before and as they hurried on their way he peered at the various doors. They all had exciting looking names on them. Some were to do with novels, and some with art books, and one was even labelled COOK BOOKS – TEST KITCHEN.

"That's where we try out all our recipes," explained the girl, as she saw Paddington licking his lips. She pointed to the room next door. "But I'm sure this is much more your cup of tea."

Paddington peered up at the notice. It said GUIDE BOOKS EDITOR: but before he had time to reply he was ushered in and found himself being greeted by a man in a smart blue suit.

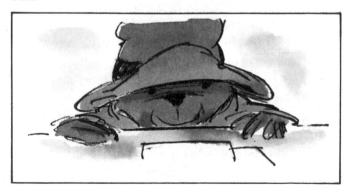

"I'm so glad you could come," boomed the man, pumping Paddington's paw up and down. "We're all tremendously excited by your project."

"You *are*?" exclaimed Paddington excitedly. He was so taken aback at the news it was a moment or two before he realised the man was still talking to him.

"I was asking if you had anything to show me?" repeated Mr. Fitch.

Paddington opened his suitcase. "I've brought my scrapbook," he announced. "It's got everything in it that's ever happened to me since I reached England."

Mr. Fitch leaned across his desk and clasped it reverently. "Naturally," he said, "we shall treat it with the greatest respect."

will be receiving. One doesn't like talking of these things, but . . . er . . . would ten per cent of the published price be to your liking?"

"Ten per cent!" exclaimed Paddington, nearly falling off his chair with surprise.

"Shall we say twelve and a half per cent then?" said Mr. Fitch hastily.

Paddington gave him a hard stare.

Mr. Fitch went slightly pale. "I can see you drive a hard bargain," he exclaimed, as he made an alteration to a document in front of him. "I'm afraid fifteen per cent is the highest we can possibly go."

Handing Paddington a pen, he pushed the papers across the table towards him. "Perhaps you'd like to sign now and we'll be happy to call it settled."

He placed the book on his desk and then removed an invisible speck of dust from his lapel. "Er . . . I hate to bring the subject up with a personage such as yourself," he continued, with a hint of embarrassment, "but have you had any thoughts about the royalty?"

"I think there's a bit near the beginning," said Paddington. "Mr. Gruber once took me to see Buckingham Palace and we thought we saw the Queen looking out of a window".

Mr. Fitch looked slightly taken aback for the moment. "I meant, of course, the money you

Mr. Fitch obviously wanted to get the whole matter completed before he was forced into paying even more, and he watched closely, if with growing surprise, as Paddington signed his name carefully and then dipped his paw into a nearby bottle of ink and pressed it on the paper.

"That's to show it's genuine," explained Paddington.

"Er, yes," said Mr. Fitch, with a nervous chuckle. "I suppose it's something you learned to do in the bush?"

"No," said Paddington. "My Aunt Lucy taught me."

Mr. Fitch began to look even more ill at ease. "Perhaps while I deal with this," he said, carefully blotting the paw print, "you would like to have a look around our premises. We have a very good map room which might interest you."

Paddington considered the matter for a moment. The long walk to Lovejoy and Fitch had given him an appetite and it was almost time for lunch anyway. "It's very kind of you," he said, "but I think perhaps I would really rather see your test kitchen?"

"Ah, I expect you're thinking of some Peruvian specialties?" suggested Mr. Fitch.

"Well, no," said Paddington. "I'd be quite happy with some cocoa and buns."

Mr. Fitch stood up and opened the door. "I'm afraid Miss Ann Gelica our cooking expert is off sick at the moment," he explained, as he led the way into the next room. "I think she was having trouble with her 'petit fours' yesterday. What one might call an occupational hazard," he added hastily as he caught Paddington's hard stare. "If you don't mind I'll leave you to your own devices for a few moments while I get copies of the contract made."

"Oh, I don't mind at all, Mr. Fitch," said Paddington gratefully. "I like being left to my own devices and I've never been in a test kitchen before."

Whatever it was that had befallen Loveday and Fitch's cookery expert seemed to have stricken her rather suddenly, for the table in the center of the room was still littered with the remains of the dish she'd been preparing.

The sight of all the food made Paddington feel even more hungry and as soon as the door had closed behind him he picked up a cook book and hastily turned the pages until he reached the part marked B for Buns.

Gathering all the ingredients together, he soon set to work. Into a large mixing bowl he poured a generous helping of flour, made a well in the center, and then added some special milk and yeast mixture, followed by two eggs,

butter, salt, and a teaspoon of allspice and cinnamon for good measure.

The recipe spoke about kneading the bun mixture and by then Paddington felt as if he'd never needed anything quite so much before. Already the mixture was beginning to stick to his fur in large globs, and when he mopped his brow even more transferred itself to his head, so that he had quite a job getting his hat back on. He began to wish he'd taken his duffle coat off first. Miss Gelica obviously liked working with a good deal of light and the heat from the lamps was becoming rather overpowering.

In desperation he looked around for an easier way of doing things, and as he did so his gaze alighted on a small electric mixer lying nearby.

It was then that his troubles really started. In his anxiety to get the buns into the oven before Mr. Fitch returned, Paddington made the fatal mistake of switching on the mixer *before* he put it into the bowl.

He wasn't at all sure what happened next, but as he plunged the whirring blades into the mixture, it suddenly felt as if the Heavens had opened and a tropical rainstorm was taking place. Lumps of dough shot everywhere; into his face, over the table and the shelves and the oven; onto the walls, and even up onto the ceiling, where they hung for a moment or two like strange white stalactites before falling with a dull thud to the floor.

It was while the excitement was at its height that the door suddenly opened and Mr. Fitch reappeared. He was accompanied by a tall, bronzed man with a beard and they both stood for a moment, transfixed by the sight which met their eyes.

"Perhaps," said the stranger with an air of authority as he stepped into the room, "it would be better if you unplugged the mixer."

Paddington looked up gratefully as the man pulled the plug and the motor came to a stop.

He'd been so surprised by what had happened that he hadn't time to even think about taking the mixer out of the bowl, let alone switch it off.

Mr. Fitch gazed around the room in horror. "I don't know what Miss Gelica will say when she sees this," he wailed. Then he turned and pointed a trembling finger at Paddington. "You're an imposter! You're not Daniel Peake the famous explorer at all."

"Daniel Peake the famous explorer!" exclaimed Paddington hotly. "Certainly not! I'm Paddington Brown and I'm a bear!"

If Paddington thought that this latest piece of information would act as a soothing balm to Mr. Fitch's temper, he was doomed to disappointment. Mr. Fitch looked for a

moment as if he would have welcomed taking on the job of an explorer himself; preferably in an area of the world as far away from young Paddington Bear as possible.

"Why don't we sit down?" said the stranger, pouring oil on troubled waters. He held out his hand to Paddington. "*I'm* Daniel Peake. Just back from Darkest Peru with my new manuscript HOT FOOT THROUGH THE UPPER REACHES."

Lowering his voice he bent down until his head was level with Paddington's. "I'm tickled pink with the new royalties you've negotiated,"

Mr. Fitch gave a shudder. From the general state of the kitchen, he obviously felt that Paddington's paws would have been better in the sea rather than over it, but realising he was beaten he decided to submit with good grace.

He was about to ring for some refreshments when he caught sight of the remains of the previous day's experiments.

"How about rounding things off with some 'petit fours'?" he asked.

Daniel Peake turned to Paddington. "As one writer to another," he said, "what do you think of that as a suggestion?"

"I think it's a very good one, Mr. Peake," said Paddington. "Except I think I would prefer some 'petit fives'. So much has happened to me today I'm really very hungry indeed."

It was some time before Paddington finally left the offices of LOVEJOY AND FITCH, and later still before he'd finished explaining the day's happenings to the Browns.

"Just imagine Paddington getting into print," said Mrs. Brown, as the door finally closed behind him and he made his way up to bed clutching his scrapbook.

"All very exciting," said Mrs. Bird, "but if you ask me it's probably just as well that young bear's memoirs aren't going to see the light of day in their entirety. Thinking about some of the messes he's gotten into in his time there's no telling what ideas they might put into people's heads if they ever did get published!"

he whispered. "Wouldn't have dared ask myself."

"Look here," began Mr. Fitch.

"I was thinking of changing my publisher," continued Mr. Peake, in a slightly louder voice "But I won't now, of course."

"In fact," he added, drawing up a chair, "I've been hearing all about your scrapbook. I wouldn't mind going through it if I may. Perhaps we could add another chapter to my book – PAWS ACROSS THE SEA or something. It'll give the whole thing a new twist."

Heavens Above

Did you know that the sign of the Zodiac you were born under can play a large part in making you the type of person you are? Paddington has been studying the characteristics of each sign and trying to guess which ones all the people he knows were born under. Of course, Paddington has two birthdays each year, so he doesn't fit into any one category. But then, as everyone knows, Paddington is in a class of his own!

CAPRICORN (21 December – 19 January)
You are ambitious and know exactly where you're going. People often think you are very serious, but you have your own kind of straight-faced humour. You make a very loyal friend and have great strength of character. You never let yourself be hurried. And you have a well-earned reputation for making ends meet.

AQUARIUS (20 January – 18 February)
You are always interested in what is new – new friends, new places to go and things to do. You can easily give the impression of being aloof and stand-offish. But you are probably deep in thought, thinking up some new adventure.

PISCES (19 February – 20 March)
Your lively wit makes you popular, although you have a rather annoying habit of changing your mind every two minutes. You sometimes give the impression of being shy. But once you have finally made up your mind about something, you astound others by your self-confidence in putting your ideas across.

ARIES (21 March – 20 April)

You are impulsive – you like to do things on the spur of the moment. But you do lack patience with those who don't want to drop everything and join you! You have a lot of energy, coupled with great perseverance. Once you have made up your mind to do something you won't stop until it's done. You can lack flexibility.

CANCER (21 June – 20 July)

You have a tendency to live in the past. You are gentle by nature and will do almost anything to avoid an argument. You have very strong intuitions and may even by psychic! You are artistic and creative, and usually go out of your way to make your surroundings warm and colorful.

TAURUS (21 April – 20 May)

You love luxury and want the best of everything. You enjoy good food. You are happiest doing things with your family and friends, rather than alone. You nearly always have very strong ideas about exactly what shape your life should take. Your strength of mind is sometimes called 'stubbornness' by other people. And you are very practical.

LEO (21 July – 21 August)

You have a very strong, powerful personality and can easily be thought arrogant or vain. You have a lot of energy and drive. Instead of waiting for things to happen you go out and *make* them happen. You are very optimistic and are always prepared to give your friends the benefit of the doubt. And you are very generous.

GEMINI (21 May – 20 June)

You have a very happy-go-lucky nature. This makes you great fun to have around, although some of your more gloomy friends may get a bit tired of your eternal cheerfulness! You are very resourceful. You have to guard against people taking advantage of your good nature. But, even if they do, you are very resilient.

SCORPIO (23 October – 22 November)

You have a strong sense of humor which enables you to get over any disappointments. You can give the impression of being secretive and you don't like always to be part of a crowd. You are a wonderful friend and a bad enemy – you don't go in for half measures. You could turn out to be a Saint or a Sinner.

VIRGO (22 August – 22 September)

You tend on the whole to be very prudent. But when you feel like it you can make very extravagant gestures. You are slow to make friends because you are shy of taking the first step. But once you make a friend, you stay friends for life! You may well have a great love of books. And you are very critical.

SAGITTARIUS (23 November – 20 December)

You are definitely a 'doer' – which means that you are sometimes thought to be impatient. You are very independent and like to dash off after your own pursuits. Your zest for life makes you want to pass on some of your enthusiasm to those younger than yourself. You love travelling and feel very at home in far-flung places.

LIBRA (23 September – 22 October)

You love harmony and get on well with other people. You don't like being alone. You like nice surroundings and have very strong feelings about the sort of clothes you like to wear. You may be an escapist, loving to dream up a fantasy world of your own. And you often put off things you have to do in the real world – almost indefinitely!

Aunt Lucy's Poncho

Most of Paddington's early memories are about Peru, particularly Darkest Peru, where he was brought up by his Aunt Lucy.

Although Peru is in South America, where the climate is hot, the nights can be very cold, especially up in the mountains. Whenever

Paddington tries to picture his aunt he always sees her in his mind's eye dressed in one of the cape-like 'ponchos' that are worn in that part of the world.

You will need: a large piece of plain, brightly-colored, warm material; scissors; needle and thread; pins; embroidery threads and needle; chalk; ruler; tape measure; thick fringing for trimming.

What to do:
Take a piece of material and fold it in half like this. The bottom must be long enough to cover your middle and the sides should fall almost to your elbow. Pin the edges together. Measure round your head with a tape measure. Divide the result by two and add on 1 inch.

Now mark this length in the center of the fold with pins, as shown.

Ask a friend to measure from where your neck joins your shoulder to just below your elbow and mark this length with a pin along from each of the neck hole pins. Measure from the foot of your neck at the front to about 3 inches below your waist.

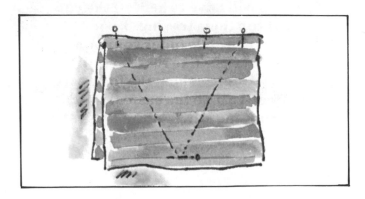

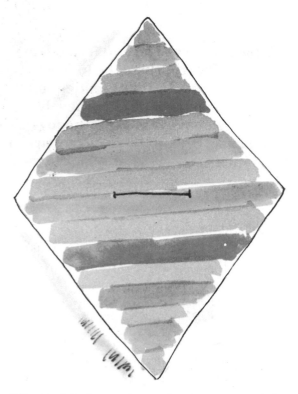

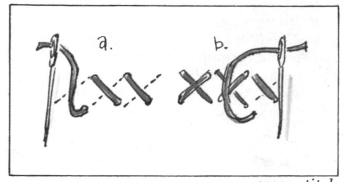

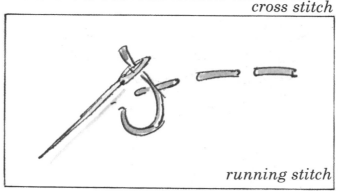

cross stitch

running stitch

Mark this length on the bottom of the material. Make sure you mark it exactly underneath the mid-point of the neck-hole (use the ruler to measure exactly).

With chalk and the ruler join up the three pins marking the sides and the foot of the poncho. Pin the two sides together along the inside of the chalk line. Now very carefully cut along the chalk lines, through both thicknesses.

Open up the material. You should have a diamond shape like this. With ruler and chalk, join up the two pins marking the neck hole. Cut along the line. Slip the poncho over your head to make sure the head hole is big enough. If you have to make it bigger, be sure to add the same amount to each side. Unless your material is felt, you will have to hem all the cut edges to stop them fraying.

Now you can embroider your poncho. Simple patterns — like two lines of diamonds running along the foot — are most effective. Use the easiest stitches, like the running stitch or the cross stitch.

You can go on to embroider your initials in satin stitch on the front if you like. Finish off by trimming the foot of your poncho with fringes. You can buy fringing ready-made — choose thick, brightly-colored fringes. Sew them all round the foot of your poncho.

61

The Portobello Road Mystery

Crouching down on all fours in front of a long wooden fence, Paddington applied his right eye carefully to a peep hole a foot or so above the sidewalk and peered through it with interest.

As it turned out it was as well he did have all four of his paws firmly on the ground, otherwise he might well have fallen over backwards with astonishment; even so, there was an awful moment or two before he finally recovered his balance well enough to be able to apply his left eye to the hole in order to make extra sure he was seeing straight.

The fence in question was part of a long one surrounding a construction site on Portobello Road and it was there to protect people from falling down the enormous hole which was behind it.

The site had been a continuing source of gossip in the neighbourhood ever since work had begun. Paddington in particular had followed progress with interest, and over the months he had struck up quite a friendship with the foreman of the building company. Several times he'd been shown around, and once he'd even been given a quick look at some

plans showing the building which was to be built very soon.

As it happened Paddington hadn't been past the site for several days, and quite a change had come over it. Normally the area was swarming with workmen, but even though dusk was falling there was still more than an hour left before quitting time, it was almost empty. In fact, the only activity came from a spot somewhere near the middle where a group of people he didn't remember ever having seen before had gathered.

They seemed to be behaving very strangely indeed. Although they weren't dressed as workmen, the central figure of the group was wielding a shovel which gleamed in the evening sun as if made of some dull but well-polished metal. Even as Paddington watched, the man put the finishing touches on a hole in the ground and as he did so another figure detached himself from the group and with the help of the others, reverently lowered what looked like a metal box into the opening.

After a brief pause the first man replaced the earth from a pile by his side and began stamping it level. Then they all shook hands,

turned, and headed towards a ladder near where Paddington was standing.

Scrambling to his feet, Paddington picked up his suitcase and hurried on his way in the direction of Windsor Gardens. The whole incident had lasted barely a minute or two and yet it felt as though it had taken ages. He sank deeper and deeper into his thoughts. On the one hand there was really nothing wrong with what had happened, and yet it was all very odd.

He couldn't for the life of him think what it could be about. One part of him wanted to tell someone about the whole thing, but really, there was nothing much to tell.

By the time he got back to the Browns' house he was very deep in thought and after a quick supper he hurried upstairs to his room where he spent some time pouring over his scrap-book writing in an account of the affair. After that he drew a map of the area on a separate sheet of paper, carefully marking in for good measure the spot where he'd seen the men burying the box, and then went to bed.

Paddington slept very fitfully that night. He had quite a few dreams, mostly to do with

digging holes, and several times he woke and lifted up the sheets in order to make sure he hadn't been lying on a shovel by accident.

The next day he was up bright and early and after a quick breakfast he grabbed his duffle coat and hat, packed his suitcase, and hurried off back down Windsor Gardens in the direction of Portobello Road in order to carry his investigation a stage further.

On reaching the site he found it was very different to when he'd left it the night before. Quite a large crowd had collected, the taller ones among them straining their necks in order to see over the top of the fence so that they could relay back information to their less fortunate companions.

"They're searching for some remains," announced one man.

"They found some the other day," said a woman pushing a stroller. "My husband is one of the builders and he says they've all had to stop work while they carry on looking for some more. A skeleton it was – all bones. Someone put their jackhammer through it by mistake. That's how they found it."

"Must have been quite shocking," said a friend sympathetically. "To think of having all those bones inside us! Makes you wonder."

The man who'd been relaying the information looked somewhat annoyed that he was being forgotten.

"Bones," he said darkly, "may not be all they find. You mark my words."

Paddington felt his fur stand on end as he listened to the conversation, and without further ado he bent down to the knot hole and applied his gaze to what was going on down below. But if he was expecting to see anything exciting he was doomed to disappointment. In fact, there was even less going on than there had been the previous evening; a few scattered tools were lying around and there were a number of freshly dug shallow trenches in the ground, but otherwise all was quiet. There was no sign at all of the people he'd seen the evening before. It was all very mysterious.

"Too late, chum" said one of the onlookers sympathetically, as he climbed down from his perch and caught Paddington's look of disappointment.

"They've all gone for their coffee break. But they'll be back again. You mark my words. They'll be back." He nodded towards two uniformed figures near the entrance gates. "You ask them. They'll tell you."

Paddington needed no second bidding. Opening his suitcase he withdrew the map he'd taken to bed the night before and then hurried along the pavement towards the policemen on duty.

"I know where there are some more bones hidden!" he announced excitedly. "There's a whole boxful. I saw them being buried last night on my way home."

At first the policeman looked as if they were all set to send Paddington away, but as they listened to the tale unfold their expressions changed.

"How many people did you say there were?" asked one of them.

"Five or six," said Paddington vaguely. "One of them dug a hole with a special shovel. Then the others put a box inside the hole and they covered it over again. It was getting dark so it was a bit difficult to see, but I know where it was because I made a special map. Look!" And he held the piece of paper up for them to see.

The policemen exchanged glances.

"Come with us," said the second one briskly.

Paddington led the way into the building site, down the ladder which the men had used the previous night, and then, with the aid of his map, hurried towards a spot clearly marked with a large 'X'.

"Good work," said the first policeman approvingly as he took in the mound of hastily smoothed-over earth.

Removing his jacket he grabbed a nearby shovel and started digging up the ground in front of him.

"Sir Reginald's going to get a shock when he hears about this," he exclaimed.

"Sir Reginald?" repeated Paddington in surprise, picking up another shovel in order to lend a paw. As far as he could remember the foreman's name was Alf, and he never seemed surprised at anything.

"Sir Reginald's in charge," explained the second policeman, pausing to mop his brow. "He's been digging up remains all the week. He is very fussy. Insists on having every bit of earth sifted in case there are any foreign bodies mixed in with it." He gave a chuckle. "So if all you say is true he's going to get more than he bargained for."

Paddington gazed uneasily at the patch of earth beneath his feet. It suddenly didn't seem as inviting as it had done a few moments before. Fortunately for his peace of mind it all looked pretty normal. In fact, apart from an old plate with some pieces chipped off the edge there was nothing unusual at all. Seeing the plate reminded Paddington that in his rush he hadn't had quite such a large breakfast as usual, so removing the object from the ground he wiped it carefully with his paw, unlocked his suitcase, and withdrew a small paper bag which he opened.

"Would you care for a marmalade sandwich?" he asked, offering the plate to the policemen.

The man eyed it distastefully. "No, thank you," said the first one. "We're not supposed to eat on duty."

He looked as if he'd been about to say more but at that moment there was a loud bellow from somewhere just behind them.

Paddington's sandwich nearly went flying, but fortunately he just managed to catch the plate in time.

He turned and then nearly jumped out of his skin with fright again as he saw an imposing-looking man wearing cotton trousers and a safari shirt standing right behind him. The man had a tanned face with a huge, bushy old-fashioned moustache which was twitching with indignation.

"That's him!" gasped Paddington. "That's one of the men I saw last night."

The first policeman gazed at him with a look of disbelief.

"That can't be!" he exclaimed. "That's Sir Reginald!"

"Sir Reginald Barlow, the archeologist," hissed the second one, as he dusted himself down. "He's famous for his digs."

Paddington backed away. The way Sir Reginald was jabbing his finger in every direction he could easily see how he'd earned his reputation.

"I'm very sorry about this, Sir Reginald," said the first policeman. "There seems to have been some mistake."

"Mistake!" boomed Sir Reginald. "*Mistake!* I'll say there's been a mistake. That's my posterity box you're just digging up. Only buried it last night. Had a special ceremony with a gold shovel to mark the occasion."

Paddington listened with growing astonishment. He'd never heard of an archeologist before, let alone one with a posterity box *and* a gold shovel.

"Perhaps," he said, holding out the plate again with a hopeful expression on his face, "you'd like a marmalade sandwich, Sir Reginald."

Paddington was a great believer in marmalade in time of trouble. In the past he'd often found that problems had a habit of solving themselves if you sat down for a quiet marmalade sandwich.

But if he thought his offer would have the desired effect of calming things down he was doomed to disappointment. Although Sir Reginald was gnashing his teeth with gusto,

from the look on his face it was clear that of the many things he might like to have buried them in, a marmalade sandwich was pretty low on the list.

"A marmalade sandwich my foot!" he spluttered. "Marmalade sandwich! Why . . ." And then the expression on his face suddenly changed.

"May I have a closer look, bear?" he exclaimed.

"Certainly," said Paddington. "I'm afraid it's a bit old, but . . ."

"Old?" repeated Sir Reginald. "I'll say it's old. Why, it must be early Roman if it's a day."

"Early Roman!" exclaimed Paddington hotly. "It was fresh this morning. Mrs. Bird would never let me eat anything *that* old."

Paddington's sandwich may have got a bit squashed in the excitement but it had been made with a new jar of marmalade from the discount grocery store, and knowing his love of marmalade they always made sure their stocks were fresh.

But to his alarm, Sir Reginald brushed the sandwich to one side.

"I am not talking about marmalade sandwiches, bear," he exclaimed. "I am talking about this!" And he held the plate up for all to

see. "This," he announced dramatically, "is what we've been looking for. An almost perfect Roman dinner plate made over two thousand years ago. The missing link in all the pieces we've found over the last few days. The last item in our collection to make a complete Roman dinner set. You may take it," he said, with simple sincerity as he held out his hand, "that Sir Reginald and the country are grateful."

"Thank you, Sir Reginald," said Paddington, still not really sure what it was all about, but not wishing to be outdone. "I'm very grateful too – at least I think I am!"

Paddington settled himself alongside Sir Reginald on the Chesterfield in Mr. Gruber's antique shop while his friend busied himself on the stove at the back making some cocoa for what had turned out to be a very delayed morning coffee break.

After all the excitement on the construction site they had adjourned to the shop for some much-needed peace and quiet.

"I think," said Sir Reginald, as Mr. Gruber handed him a steaming mug, "I'd better put you in the picture.

"You see, when they were digging the foundations for the new sky scraper they accidentally discovered some Roman remains . . . some old bones . . . and a mosaic floor. They stopped work at once and called us in so that we could see what else we could find. Putting all the bits and pieces together we decided it must have once been the site of an old Roman palace. We found all sorts of things . . . the remains of an old heating system . . . some jewelry . . . even some dice made of bone which the Roman soldiers must have played with. Bit by bit we built up a picture of life as it was back then, and we even, as I said earlier, dug up the remains of an almost complete dinner set – one of the most perfect ever found in this country.

"Beats me," he added, pointing to Paddington's plate, "how we managed to miss that. Why, we were so close we almost buried our posterity box on it last night."

"I've often found," said Mr. Gruber, "that the very thing you are looking for is often right under your nose. It's a case of not seeing the forest for the trees." He gave a cough. "I'm sure I'm speaking for young Mr. Brown as well," he continued, "when I ask what may sound like a silly question . . . but what exactly *is* a 'posterity box'?"

Sir Reginald slapped his knee. "Bless my soul!" he exclaimed. "Should have explained. They've got one under Cleopatra's Needle besides the River Thames. It's a box full of things from the present day, so that anyone who happens to dig it up in a few thousand years can see what life was like in our time, Thought I'd bury one myself. It seemed only

fair. We dug up a lot of Roman remains and in doing so learned a bit more about their way of life – so why not do something for the people who come after us." He listed the items on his fingers. "There's a newspaper of today. A picture of the Houses of Parliament. A pop record. A set of coins . . ." He broke off and stared at Paddington as a sudden thought struck him.

"Just had an idea," he said, slapping his knee again. "Seeing you found the plate for us, why

don't you bury a box of your own alongside ours?"

Paddington nearly fell off the sofa with excitement at the thought.

"I don't think I've ever buried a box for posterity before," he admitted.

"Well, you're allowed six items," said Sir Reginald, "so think carefully."

Paddington opened his suitcase and considered the matter for a moment or two. "I'm afraid bears don't have many relics, Sir Reginald," he said, "but there's a picture of the Brown family I took myself a long time ago. Then there's the page out of my scrap book telling all about how I saw you digging the hole for your box – with a special paw mark to show that it's genuine. And I could give you a copy of my accounts page so that people could learn how much it cost a bear to live in our days . . ."

Paddington paused for a moment and then held up an empty marmalade jar. "Perhaps I

could fill this with some of Mr. Gruber's cocoa to show the sort of thing we used to drink?" he suggested.

Mr. Gruber chuckled. "I'm not sure if it will taste very good in another two thousand years' time, Mr. Brown," he said. "Still," he pointed to the unfinished snack, "while you're doing it you could donate what's left on the tray. You could stick a label on it saying 'A typical bun of the period'."

"Capital!" Sir Reginald jumped to his feet. "I shall have another box made up this very day. Has to be air-tight as well as waterproof, you know. Wouldn't work if things got soggy.

"After all," he added, "quite a lot of people have done this sort of thing, but I don't suppose that in a few thousand years' time there'll be many boxes of bears' relics around. We must make sure they're well preserved."

"All's well that ends well," said Mr. Gruber. "And at least we have all the loose ends tied up on the Portobello Road Mystery."

"All but one," corrected Sir Reginald. "I asked this young bear for *six* items. So far he's only come up with five."

All eyes turned to Paddington.

He examined the remains of his marmalade sandwich. What with one thing and another it had taken quite a severe buffeting during the day. In fact, it was barely recognisable as any sort of sandwich, let alone a marmalade one. A number of chunks had fallen out, the middle looked very soggy indeed, and the little that was left was now covered in a film of dust from Sir Reginald's dig.

He reached a decision.

"I think," he announced, "that I would like to donate this if I may. I think if this is found in two thousand years' time it will be one of the biggest Portobello Mysteries of all!"

Paddington was allowed to bury six items for posterity. If you were given the same chance what six items would you choose to show future inhabitants of this world what life was like in our time?

69

PADDINGTON IN FOCUS

Paddington was delighted to receive a camera as a special birthday present from the Browns. He was eager to try his paw at photography at once, and take lots of snapshots to stick into his scrapbook to send to his Aunt Lucy in Peru. He soon found, however, that there is more to taking photographs than just aiming the camera and pressing the button. Here are the very first pictures that Paddington took. You can learn from his mistakes, and improve your own photography by studying these pictures.

A lovely picture of Mrs. Bird's feather duster and right foot! This was to have been an action shot of Mrs. Bird spring-cleaning. Unfortunately Paddington was too slow, and Mrs. Bird has almost cleaned her way right out of the picture!

Mr. Brown relaxing in a deckchair with his newspaper. He seems to have huge feet and a tiny head because Paddington held the camera far too close to the ground.

Jonathan has a sunflower growing out of his head! No, he hasn't let Paddington's gardening hints on page 76 go to his head. The sunflower is growing behind him; Paddington should have asked him to move to one side a bit; then we would have seen them both properly.

A very nice portrait of Mrs. Brown is ruined because Paddington had the tip of his paw in front of the lens when he pressed the button.

A picture of Mr. Gruber outside his shop. It may look like midnight, but it was actually lunch-time. Paddington forgot to take the protective cover off his camera lens.

A group of Paddington's friends from the Portobello Market. The trouble was, nobody wanted to be left out. To make sure of getting everyone in, Paddington moved much too far back. Now we cannot recognize anyone!

Mr. Curry. No, he wasn't trembling from fear that Paddington might ask him to *pay* for the portrait. Paddington (and the camera) moved as he pressed the button with his paw.

This artistic still-life 'cocoa and buns' was ruined because Paddington didn't hold the camera straight. (Paddington says he was in a hurry to finish the photograph before the cocoa got cold.)

Most cameras today have an automatic timer so that you can take a picture of yourself. You set the camera, and then you have about eight seconds in which to get into your position. Unfortunately, Paddington didn't look through the viewfinder first to make sure all of him would be in the picture.

Don't worry, Judy hasn't got mumps! Her face is distorted because Paddington held the camera much too close to her.

A perfect picture of the Brown family. At least Paddington is a bear who learns from his mistakes!

One day Paddington was out shopping when he saw a notice in a shop window.

Paddington liked a bargain, and it sounded like a great bargain.

So he decided to investigate the matter right away.

'A very good choice, sir,' said the salesman. 'I can just picture it.'

'Close your eyes, and I will tell you about it.'

Paddington was tired after his shopping and he needed no second bidding.

'On the first day,' said the man, 'I see you in Paris, climbing the Eiffel tower.'

'On the second day – Spain, with a visit to a bullfight.'

'Then Venice, with a romantic trip round the canals on a gondola.'

'Followed by climbing the Matterhorn in Switzerland; ending up on the fifth day . . .

. . . skiing in Austria. Only two hundred bucks! How's that for a real deal?'

Paddington rubbed his eyes. 'I'd rather have a day at Brightsea!' he exclaimed.

'It's a lot cheaper and much, much safer. I can go with Mr. Gruber.'

'If you close your eyes I'll tell you all about it.'

'I can just picture it!'

Sunflowers

As you probably know, Paddington was brought up by his Aunt Lucy in Darkest Peru. In some parts of Peru, huge plants sprout up and grow to great heights without any help from anyone. So when Paddington came to live with the Browns at 32 Windsor Gardens, he was very interested to see Mr. Brown's garden. Mr. Brown spent quite a lot of time there at certain times of the year, doing various important-looking things with tools, stakes and bits of twine. And yet the plants never grew as tall as the ones in Peru which were left to their own devices. Paddington thought easily the most impressive-looking plants were Mr. Brown's sunflowers. He thought they were very well named as they reminded him of the bright Peruvian sun. Mr. Brown said they very very easy to grow too. If you have a garden, why not try growing some for yourself?

Sunflowers are best planted against a wall or fence, in a sunny, sheltered place. They are grown from seed. You can buy a pack of seeds at a gardening store; their proper, Latin name is *Helianthus* but just ask for the giant, old-fashioned kind. Sow the seeds in the spring in groups of three, 15 inches apart, where you want the flowers to grow. When the plants appear above the surface, weed out two of every three seedlings, leaving the strongest with

plenty of room to grow. In dry weather, remember to water the plants often. A little liquid fertilizer — which can also be bought at gardening stores — will make them grow extra strong and tall. When the plants have grown up a bit, it is a good idea to tie them to stakes, driven in the soil beside them, for support. In the summer the sunflowers should grow to a height of 7 fcct or more! They don't have any smell to speak of, which Paddington says is just as well as the flowers are far too far up for his nose to reach! Not only are sunflowers amazingly large flowers, they are 'good value' in other ways too. When they are fully grown, you will see that in the center

of each flower is a tight cluster of striped seeds. You can use these in several ways:

1. Store them carefully and plant them next spring for more sunflowers. You will have enough to share among your friends.

2. If you have a hamster as a pet, he will love eating the seeds. You can try eating them yourself. Crack the outer casing, and chew the soft 'kernel' inside. It's quite an unusual taste, and although Mrs. Bird says they contain sunflower oil which will make his fur glossy, Paddington doesn't think they'll ever take the place of marmalade sandwiches!

3. Use the seeds to make an 'everlasting sunflower' to hang on a wall to remind you of summer:

You will need:
A large piece of white Brisol board; bright yellow crepe paper; glue; scissors; thick green poster paint; a compass and a pencil; sunflower seeds.

What to do:
With a compass, draw a pencil circle for the flower center, as shown. Paint a green stalk down from the center, and add a few leaves. Leave to dry. Cut out 30 tapering petals (4½ ins. long) from the crepe paper. Glue the base of 15 of them round the circle. Leave to dry. Now glue on the other 15, over the joins of the first 15. Leave to dry. Cover the flower centre with glue. Immediately press on lots of sunflower seeds. Gently shake off any loose ones.

You can buy a small plain calendar at a department store very cheaply. If you attach this to the bottom of the card with two small strips of ribbon, and add a ribbon loop at the top, you have a lovely sunny Christmas present.

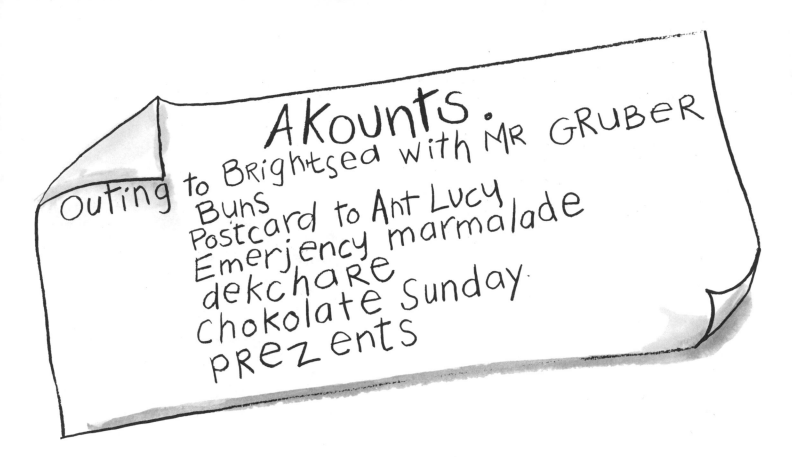

Akounts.

Outing to Brightsea with MR GRUBER

Buns

Postcard to Ant Lucy

Emerjency marmalade

dekchare

chokolate Sunday.

PREZents

This is a page of Paddington's 'Akounts', which he usually keeps safely in the secret compartment of his suitcase. As you can see, it shows his expenses during a day's outing to Brightsea with his friend Mr. Gruber. The outing turned out to be rather expensive, and Paddington was left with very little bun money for the rest of the week. He told Mr. Gruber this over their usual coffee break of cocoa and buns a few days later. Mr. Gruber was very sympathetic. In fact, he showed Paddington two ways in which he could have saved some of his bun money for other things – like more chocolate sundaes!

A very expensive item on Paddington's list was presents, as he had brought back something for all the Browns. Mr. Gruber showed him how he could have made presents from something he could get for nothing at Brightsea – pebbles.

Mr. Gruber had a box of pebbles at the back of the shop, which he brought out.

You will need:

thick, bright poster paints; a brush; clear varnish; and plenty of newspapers to spread around to catch any drips.

The trick is to find pebbles with bumps, which look as if they could be something else. 'I'll show you what I mean,' said Mr. Gruber.

He produced a squat rectangular pebble with a ridge along the top. Paddington watched with interest as he painted four black window frames and a green door on the front, and bright red tiles on top. Then he painted **32** on the front door, and added a small green shrub beside it. He left the background unpainted for a 'stone' effect.

Paddington saw that the pebble had turned into a model of 32 Windsor Gardens, where he lived.

'It's important to leave it until it's dry. Then clean your brush and paint the pebble with clear varnish,' said Mr. Gruber. 'This makes it very shiny and stops the paint rubbing off.' Paddington thought this would make a very good present for Mr. Brown. He could use it as a paperweight.

'It will stop important papers blowing off his desk,' agreed Mr. Gruber.

Mr. Gruber then produced a pebble with a hole in it. He outlined the hole in red, added eyes, a nose and some hair. And there was a funny face!

If you can't find pebbles that give you ideas, you can make a pretty paperweight or ornament from a plain round pebble painted with a bright pattern.

On his next visit to Brightsea, Paddington found a pebble that was just the right shape for a model of his Aunt Lucy in her bowler hat and colorful poncho.

Mr. Gruber thought Paddington could also have saved money on the picture postcard he sent to Aunt Lucy.

'After all,' he said, 'she must have quite a lot of postcards of Brightsea by now. You could send her a truly original postcard using real Brightsea sand.'

You need: a plain postcard; glue or paste; a brush; fine sand.

What to do:
With the brush, paint a pattern on the card. While the paint is still wet cover the postcard with sand. Shake off any loose sand. You will be left with a sand-patterned postcard. Paddington decided to send his Aunt Lucy a postcard with a sand paw-mark on it.

'She will know at once who it's from,' he explained.

'If it's going all the way to Darkest Peru,' said Mr. Gruber, 'it would be a good idea to spray your finished card with clear varnish, so that the sand doesn't rub off.'

Paddington Chunks

"Won't take a minute, sir," said the photographer, disappearing behind a black cloth at the back of the camera. "Just watch the birdie."

But it was as he peered at the last item that a strange expression suddenly came over Paddington's face. He breathed heavily on his glasses several times, polished them with a piece of rag which he took out of his suitcase, and then looked through them again at the board.

"That's called a selection from Schubert's *Unfinished Symphony*," explained Judy in a whisper.

"What!" exclaimed Paddington hotly as his worst suspicions were confirmed. "Mr. Gruber's paid a dollar each for our tickets and they haven't even finished it!"

from ***Paddington at Large***

Paddington looked around. There was no bird in sight that he could see. He went round behind the man and tapped him. The photographer, who appeared to be looking for something, jumped and then emerged from under his cloth. "How do you expect me to take your picture if you don't stand in front? Now I've wasted a plate, and" – he looked shiftily at Paddington – "that will cost you fifty cents!"

Paddington gave him a hard stare. "You said there was a bird," he said. "And there wasn't."

"Well I guess it flew away when it saw your face," said the man nastily. "Now where's my fifty cents?"

Paddington looked at him even harder for a moment. "Perhaps the bird took it when it flew away," he said.

from ***A Bear Called Paddington***

"Come on, Paddington," Mr. Brown called, as the waiter set light to the pan. "Come and see Mr. Gruber's omelette. It's on fire."

"What!" cried Paddington, poking his head out from under the table. "Mr. Gruber's omelete's on fire?"

He stared in astonishment at the waiter as he bore the silver tray with its flaming omelete towards the table.

"It's all right, Mr. Gruber," he called, waving his paws in the air. "I'm coming!"

Before the Browns could stop him, Paddington had grabbed his paw bowl and thrown the contents over the tray. There was a loud hissing noise and before the astonished gaze of the waiter Mr. Gruber's omelete slowly collapsed into a soggy mess in the bottom of the dish.

Several people near the Browns applauded. "What an unusual idea," said one of them. "Having the cabaret act sit at one of the tables just like anyone else."

from ***Paddington Helps Out***

"I thought you said that bear was going to the Peruvian Embassy?" exclaimed the bus conductor.

"The Peruvian Embassy?" repeated Mrs. Brown indignantly. "We certainly said no such thing."

"But you said she was C.D.," broke in the Inspector. "That stands for *Corps Diplomatique*, and people in the Diplomatic Corps are entitled to special treatment. That's why we brought her here."

"No," said Mrs. Bird, as light began to dawn. "We didn't say C.D. We simply said she was feeling *seedy*. That's quite a different matter."

from ***Paddington On Top***

Paddington sat up in bed holding a thermometer in his paw. "I think I must have caught the measles, Mrs. Bird," he announced weakly. "My temperature's over one hundred and twenty!"

"One hundred and twenty!" Mrs. Bird hurriedly examined the thermometer. "That's not a temperature," she exclaimed with relief. "That's a marmalade stain."

from ***Paddington At Work***

83

All is Revealed

Paddington has been looking at an old book he found in the Brown's bookcase called *Fortune Telling. The Secrets of the Orient Revealed.* If you cross his paw with silver, he may reveal some of the secrets to you too.

Reading cups

This is very interesting because tea leaves always make quite different patterns. When you have only the dregs left in your teacup, swirl them round three times. Now quickly turn the cup upside down onto the saucer. Of course it doesn't work if you make your tea with bags. Paddington tried it once with the cocoa grounds left in the bottom of his mug, but the only 'message' he got was a rather fierce one from Mrs. Bird when she saw the tablecloth!

The tea leaves make various shapes inside the cup. The nearer to the rim of the cup the shapes are, the sooner the things they predict will happen. Here is a useful list of shapes and what they mean. Initials stand for people you know.

Ace change
Anchor a journey
Arrow danger
Balloon good luck if it's going up; bad luck if it's coming down. (And it's cheating to turn the cup upside down and give it a thump on the bottom!)
Basket present or visitor (both if you're lucky!)
Bee hard work
Beehive good luck
Bird good news
Candle help is on its way
Cat watch out for someone taking advantage of you
Clouds trouble
Cup a reward
Dog a good friend
Egg new scheme – you're hatching a new idea!
Envelope news
Flag news from far away
Flower you get something you've asked for
Gate happiness
Glove a challenge; someone is throwing down the gauntlet!
Gun trouble to be avoided
Hammer work
Key a new project
Kite a wish will be granted
Knife you may argue with a friend
Ladder success
Lion a quarrel
Moon riches
Mountain an obstacle in your path
Musical notes good luck
Owl bad luck
Parrot gossip
Profile new friend
Sailor someone is coming home

Ship travel – with something gained at the end of it
Spider reward for work done
Star very lucky: health, wealth and happiness
Tent you'll wander
Tree happiness
Violin independence
Waterfall a sign of plenty
Window your happiness is at home
X someone upsets you
Zebra foreign travel

So, if Paddington's teacup looked like this . . .

It is likely that he would receive a postcard from Aunt Lucy (flag: news from far away near her initial); make a new friend (profile), come into some unexpected bun money (moon: riches), and he should be very careful where he puts any new marmalade stains, or he could end up in trouble with Mrs. Bird (gun: trouble to be avoided).

Reading cards

According to fortune tellers, each card in a pack has a meaning, and can be used to foretell the future. Shuffle the pack well. Ask the person whose fortune is to be told to cut the pack seven times. Then arrange the top seven cards in a line and 'read' them with the meanings given below as a guide. Try to link up the meanings of the seven cards, rather than just reading each one in isolation.

Hearts

Ace a gift from a friend
2 a visit from a friend
3 useful advice is on its way
4 you have plans to improve your surroundings
5 an invitation
6 a special outing
7 travel plans
8 look out for a friend who is envious of something you've got
9 someone far away gets in touch
10 someone shows appreciation of you by giving you a present
Jack a stranger brings excitement into your life
Queen a mother, an aunt, a teacher (or some other woman) is very helpful with one of your schemes.
King you can turn to some older man, in a position of authority, for advice

Diamonds

Ace good advice leads to a gain
2 it will help you to discuss any money problems with family and friends
3 people don't appreciate you
4 beware of extravagance!
5 a trip or outing gives you lots of opportunities for spending
6 something you make brings money
7 a windfall from an older person
8 you need some extra money. Don't be shy about asking for it.
9 take a chance: it will pay off
10 act quickly and make a gain
Jack a stranger, whom you will soon meet, will be very lucky for you where money is concerned
Queen an older woman will help you with a practical problem
King an older man gives you the opportunity to earn some spare cash

Spades

Ace   there are problems ahead; don't take any risks

2   be very cautious

3   you will be involved in a quarrel

4   be very careful whose advice you take

5   don't listen to gossip

6   a minor setback in one of your plans

7   don't be jealous: it will only harm yourself

8   don't take any important decisions just now; wait a while

9   you will get a letter soon which will help you make up your mind about something

10   after a lot of delays you will finally achieve what you want

Jack   someone is having a bad influence on you

Queen   some woman you know is unlucky for you

King   some man whom you trust and look up to is not a real friend

Clubs

Ace   temporary delays in something you've planned

2   you make a mistake in something

3   you will change your mind about something

4   you should concentrate on your home and family just now

5   don't rush into something

6   a bit of dull plodding is necessary at this time

7   don't be afraid to try something new: you'll be very successful

8   have some patience: something you're hoping for will happen soon

9   look after your belongings: there is a danger of losing something

10   plans for your future are taking shape

Jack   someone you know tries to persuade you to go on a holiday or trip. You will enjoy it if you go.

Queen   a very good friend will help you out of difficulties

King   a man will come to the rescue during a dull or unhappy period

These are the cards which Paddington chose.
Can you tell what his fortune is to be?

Seeing Stars

Brown?" asked Mr. Gruber, stopping for a rest and mopping his brow absent-mindedly with a large duster. "I bought this old brass telescope at an auction yesterday and it needs a good rub." He went off to get the cocoa mugs. "If you would like to borrow the telescope tonight," said Mr. Gruber, reappearing with the tray, "you can look through it and see a great Bear." Paddington was so surprised he nearly fell off the Chesterfield. But Mr. Gruber explained that the Great Bear was the name of a group of stars – or constellation. "The Ancient Greeks gave the constellations the names by which they're still known today," he said. "Do the stars look like a bear?" asked Paddington. "I suppose they do if you use a bit of imagination," said Mr.Gruber, taking a dusty book down from a shelf behind him. While Paddington enjoyed his cocoa and put his

One morning when Paddington stopped off at Mr. Gruber's shop on Portobello Road for his usual cocoa and buns, he found his friend hard at work. He was polishing what looked like a long, heavy tube. "Is it break time already, Mr.

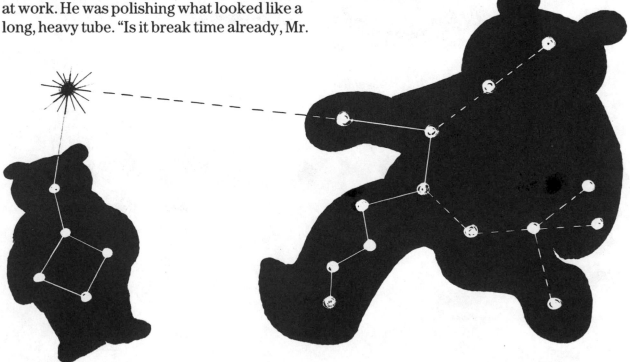

paws up, Mr. Gruber made some notes and drawings on a large piece of paper. Here are some of the things he showed Paddington.

Although all the stars appear to move around the sky, there is one star – called the North Star – which appears to remain still. This star shows the direction of the North Pole. If you live north of the Equator you can easily find the North Star. It is part of a group of stars called the Little Dipper. The easiest way to find the North Star is to look for the Big Dipper, which is part of the Great Bear. If you follow an imaginary line from the two end stars of the Big Dipper you come to the North Star. If you can find the North Star you will always know which direction is North. So you should never get lost.

Paddington says it's quite easy to get lost, even if you do know where North is; especially if you've set out for somewhere, stopped for a quick snack and forgotten the address!

This is the view of the night sky Paddington's Aunt Lucy has from her room in the Home for Retired Bears in Lima, Darkest Peru. You will have the same view if you live south of the Equator. Aunt Lucy can't see the Great Bear. But as she is surrounded by bears anyway, she doesn't really mind.

Paddington's 20 Questions

Choose the answer you think is correct, and count up your score at the end.

1 Paddington's favorite snack is:
a) toast and honey
b) chocolate pudding
c) marmalade sandwiches
d) pumpkin pie

2 Paddington has buns and cocoa with his friend Mr. Gruber:
a) at morning break time
b) at afternoon tea time
c) on Saturday mornings
d) on Labor Day outings

3 Mr. Gruber calls Paddington:
a) Paddington
b) Paddy
c) Old Bear!
d) Mr. Brown

4 Paddington's Aunt Lucy lives in:
a) Australia
b) England
c) Peru
d) Mexico

5 Paddington's Aunt Lucy wears:
a) a sou'wester
b) a bowler hat
c) a sunbonnet
d) a woolly hat with a pom-pom

6 Paddington keeps notes:
a) in a diary
b) in a scrapbook
c) in an old exercise book
d) on a chart on his bedroom wall

7 The Incas – the ancient people of Peru – worshipped:
a) a huge golden statue of a bear
b) a beautiful goddess
c) the mountains
d) the sun

8 Paddington's hat was:
a) bought at Barkridge's Sale
b) an old one of Mr. Brown's
c) his Uncle's
d) a Christmas present from Mr. Gruber

9 Paddington's Aunt Lucy taught him:
a) a special hard stare
b) a double somersault
c) how to sing the Peruvian national anthem
d) how to make and embroider ponchos

10 The Browns' housekeeper is called:
a) Mrs. Fox
b) Mrs. Bird
c) Mrs. Bull
d) Mrs. Finch

11 Paddington wears:
a) a mackintosh
b) a cape
c) a duffle coat
d) a parka

12 To help him with his shopping, Paddington uses:
a) a basket on wheels
b) a suitcase
c) a string bag
c) an old carrier bag

13 The Browns first met Paddington:
a) on holiday in Peru
b) at the zoo
c) on the beach at Brightsea
d) outside the Lost Property office at Paddington Station

14 Paddington lives at:
a) 6 Portobello Road
b) 26 Victoria Place
c) 32 Windsor Gardens
d) 18 Railway Cuttings

15 How many birthdays does Paddington have each year?
a) 1
b) 2
c) 3
d) 4

16 Mr. Brown:
a) is a stationmaster
b) works in the City
c) owns a bunshop
d) has a stall in the Portobello Market

17 Paddington's Aunt Lucy sends him:
a) letters
b) telegrams
c) tape recordings
d) postcards

18 Mr. Curry, the Browns' next-door neighbour, is:
a) mean and bad-tempered
b) generous to a fault
c) very friendly – always popping in and out
d) extremely absent-minded

19 The Capital of Darkest Peru is:
a) Stow-On-The-Wold
b) Santiago
c) Lima
d) Brussels

20 Paddington's very first adventure at the Browns' home was with:
a) a lawnmower
b) a bath
c) a pan of toffee
d) a vacuum cleaner

Answers:
1: c); **2:** a); **3:** d); **4:** c); **5:** b); **6:** b); **7:** d); **8:** c); **9:** a); **10:** b); **11:** c); **12:** a); **13:** d); **14:** c); **15:** b); **16:** b); **17:** d); **18:** a); **19:** c); **20:** b).

Score:
15 – 20: Excellent! Have a bun to celebrate.
10 – 15: Fair. Have half a bun!
Under 10: You've obviously still got quite a few of Paddington's adventures to find out about!

Room for Ideas

Paddington was busy scratching out the words "At a lewse end" in his scrapbook and was adding, in large capital letters, the ominous ones: "DECKERATING MY NEW ROOM." (*More About Paddington*)

Here are some ways in which you can brighten up the walls in your room, and your door – without any of the dire results which Paddington achieved when he tried his paw at decorating!

Make Your Mark

You need:
a very large piece of white paper; ruler; pencil; felt-tip pens

What to do
Mark the paper into squares as shown. The simplest way to do this is to fold the paper in half a few times. If you fold the paper in half four times, pressing down on the folds

each time, when you open it up you will have sixteen squares. Outline the squares with a ruler and pencil. Attach the paper to your bedroom wall. Keep some colored felt pens nearby. Whenever a friend comes to visit, ask him or her to 'decorate' a square – with a drawing, poem, joke or anything you like. In time you will have a very original poster.

Family Tree
You need:
a large piece of stiff cardboard; pencil; poster paints; photographs of your family – the older the better; double-sided sticky tape.

What to do
Draw a large tree on the card. With fairly thick poster paint, color the trunk brown and the foliage a bright green. Leave it to dry. Collect photographs of your family and relatives as babies or young children.

Stick these to the tree with small pieces of double-sided tape on the back. People should have fun trying to recognize who is who!

Picture

Most junk shops and second-hand record shops have dusty piles of old sheet music which you can buy very cheaply. Paddington's friend, Mr. Gruber, has a pile in his shop on Portobello Road. The top sheets of popular songs usually have the title in lovely ornate lettering. If you look through these piles you can often find a title which looks attractive, or amusing, framed and hung on a wall.

Examples: 'Beautiful Dreamer' above a bed. 'You Were Never Lovelier' beside a mirror! 'Oh What a Beautiful Morning', or 'Stormy Weather' beside a window.

Nameplate

You need:
a piece of card long enough to take your first name with letters about 3 inches high; a pile of old magazines and newspapers; scissors; pencil; rubber; glue; brightly colored sticky tape.

What to do
Go through the pile of magazines and newspapers and cut out lots of letters for each letter in your first name. For example if your name is Judy you will cut out lots of Js Us Ds and Ys. Try to find letters in as many different sizes and colors as possible. Now draw the outline of the letters in your name on the card in pencil. Glue the cut-out letters inside the large letters as shown. Fill up the letters as closely as possible. When the glue is dry, carefully rub out the pencil outline. Frame the edges of the nameplate with brightly colored sticky tape and add a little loop to the back of the sign with which to hang it on the outside of your door.

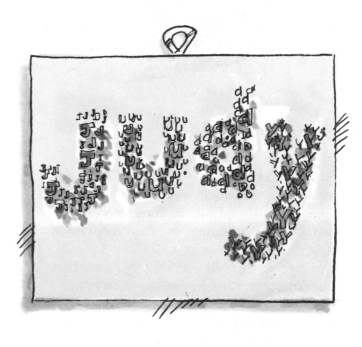

Fun for Kids

Perhaps you have a small brother or sister, or know some very young children. Here are some ideas which Paddington suggests might entertain them.

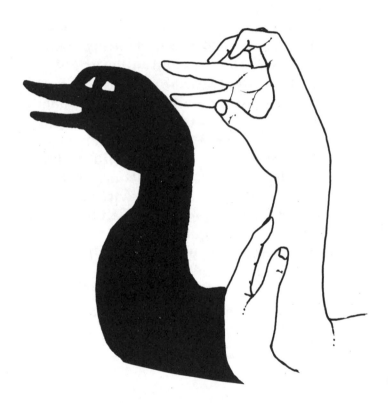

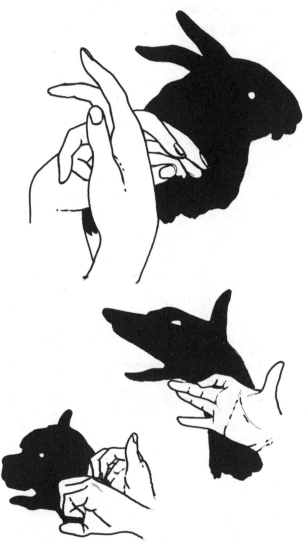

Shadow Show

Paddington says a Shadow Show is always popular – and is very good value as you don't need any special materials. All you need is a large piece of white paper stuck to the wall, or an area of white wall; a strong light (such as a powerful torch) which you shine on your 'screen'. You stand between the light and the screen. Before the show, practice some of the shapes shown here. Ducks and rabbits are always favorites with young children. With a little preparation , you can read a short story about Jemima Puddleduck or Brer Rabbit, and illustrate your story with shadow characters. (Ask at your local library for books about these two characters.) With practice you can present lots of different stories with a whole variety of animal characters.

Circular Paddington Jigsaw

You need:
a large piece of white paper
a large piece of stiff card
bright poster paints
a pencil
a compass
scissors and glue

What to do
Set your compass to 4 inches. Draw a pencil circle with them on both the paper and the card. Then draw a picture of Paddington onto the paper, inside the circle. Don't forget his duffel coat, wellingtons and hat! Make the picture as big as possible. Now paint the picture with poster paints, mixed fairly thickly to give good strong colors. Fill in the background with a bright color, such as scarlet, making sure that every bit of the paper is covered. Leave until the paint dries. Then glue the paper onto the card, making sure it fits exactly. (If necessary, trim the card.) Now draw a simple jigsaw design on top. Next cut along the lines of your design to make the jigsaw pieces. Be very careful not to snip off any edges or the pieces won't fit. For a special finish, paint the pieces with clear varnish.

Bubbles
Young children love chasing bubbles and trying to catch them. You can make your own bubble kit.

You need:
a small clean screw-top jar (such as an old coffee jar)
washing-up liquid
some wire

What to do
Put a couple of generous squeezes of the dish washing liquid into the jar. Add water until the jar is about two-thirds full of the mixture. Put the top on and shake gently. Bend the wire into the shape shown here. Make sure that the bigger loop is not too big to go through the neck of the jar. Twist the ends of the loops round the stem so that there are no sharp edges sticking out. To make bubbles, simply dip the wire loop into the mixture, take it out, and blow gently through the loop.

Paddington Mobile

This is something which will appeal to the very youngest children. Even babies get bored, and a Paddington Mobile will keep them amused for hours.

You need:
3 pieces of strong wire, each 4 inches long
1 piece of wire, 6 inches long (Ask a grown-up to cut these lengths for you).
transparent nylon thread or fishing line
fine stiff card or Bristol board
poster paints
pencil and scissors
clear varnish and a brush

What to do
Draw five shapes onto the card. They should all be roughly the same size (about 3 inches across). For example, you could draw: a bun with icing and a cherry on top; a shiny wellington boot; a bright red P for Paddington; a jar of marmalade; Paddington's hat.

Cut out the shapes. Paint them with thick poster paints, on *both* sides (letting one side dry before you do the other side). When the paint is dry, paint your shapes again with clear varnish. Make a small hole at the top of each shape. Attach a length of nylon thread or fishing line to each one, then tie them to the ends of the pieces of wire. Attach a long piece of thread to the top piece of wire with a strong knot. Your mobile probably won't hang properly at first, but you can slide the knots from side to side until it is all balanced. Hang the mobile where the baby can see it easily as it moves gently in the air.

Getting Ahead

The **Legionbear** has gone off to a life of adventure in the desert. He has left all behind him – except an emergency supply of marmalade sandwiches, of course!

The **Astrobear** zooms through space on his special mission. When he puts the first pawprint on the moon, it will be a small step for Astrobear, but a giant leap for all Earthbears.

The **Highwaybear** was notorious for his sudden raids on coaches. The unhappy passengers were made to 'stand and deliver' all the buns they had brought for the journey.

The **Swagbear** camps by a billabong. He keeps a wary eye open for kangaroos, which might swipe his billycan of cocoa. They would be told to hop it!

The **Bear Musketeers** fought duels to defend their king from all his enemies. To be chosen as a Musketeer was a real feather in any bear's cap.

The **Incabear** lived long ago in darkest Peru, high up in the Andes mountains. Aunt Lucy is very envious of Incabear's splendid hat of gold.

Beau Bear is very proud of his large wardrobe of fine clothes. He employs a valetbear specially to remove marmalade stains from his breeches.

Paddington's Great Train Race

A Board Game for 2-4 Players

For this game you need:
dice
a shaker (an eggcup will do)
up to 4 counters (you can make your own; see
foot of page)

The object of the game is to be first in a race
from START to the station at the end of your
line. Two, three or four can play. Each player
has a different color, yellow, green, red or blue.
Place your counter on the first square of your
color, where it says START.

Take it in turns to throw the dice.
Remember: you must throw a six to start.

When you have thrown a six, throw again
right away, and move forward the number of
squares shown by the dice (for example if you
throw a three, move forward three squares).

The Counters
To make your own counters, draw a circle
about ¾ of an inch in diameter on a piece of
stiff card, and cut it out. Perhaps you can find a
coin the right size. Draw around it to make
your circle. You need one counter for each
player. You should make four for this game.
Paint them in bright colors – red, green, yellow
and blue.

On each track there is a square with an
'obstacle'. If you land here, you must go back to
START. Then wait your turn to play again – at
least you don't have to throw a six this time to
get re-started!

Once you are through the smoke from Mr.
Curry's bonfire, you will see ahead that the
tracks cross. If you land on the square where
the tracks cross, go back to the square *just
before the smoke.* Then wait your turn and start
again from there. To finish, you must throw the
exact number needed. The first person to
reach home is the winner.

FINISH

FINISH

FINISH

FINISH

112

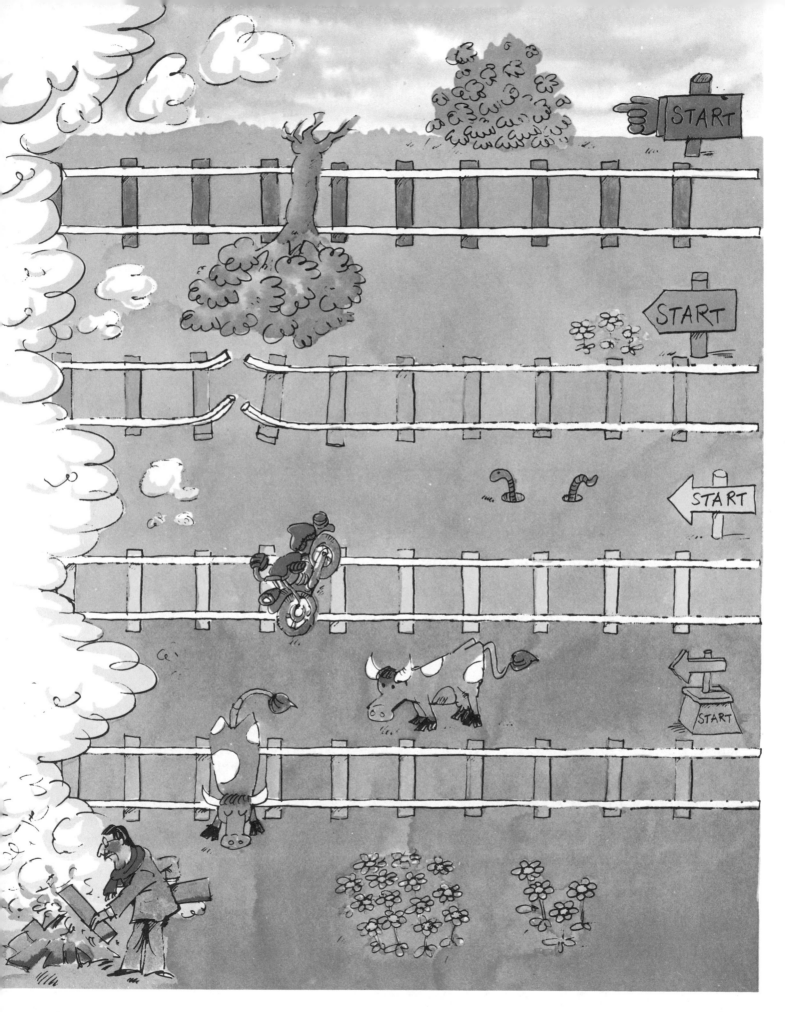

Most people, especially children, love a puppet show. It can be even more fun if you put on the show yourselves. You can make the puppets, build the theatre, and even write a 'play' for your puppets to perform. Here are some ideas to get you started. There is a short play using the characters here, on pages 118 and 119.

You need:

strong card	sticky tape
paints or crayons	tracing paper
sticks	a pencil and scissors

To make the puppets

To give you some practice, here are four 'shapes' – Paddington, Mr. Brown, Mrs. Brown and Aunt Lucy. Don't cut these out of the book – you'll want them again, or someone else will want them. Instead trace round the shapes, stick your tracing paper onto card, then cut the shape of the character out of the card. Paint the characters as has been done here. Now attach a stick to the *back* of each puppet with sticky tape, as shown. Remember to leave

enough stick for your hand to hold comfortably. Once you've got the hang of making stick puppets this way, you can make them any size or shape you like. They can be people or animals. You can start by tracing them from pictures in magazines, for example, or you can draw your character straight onto the card.

To make the theater

You can make your theater to any design you like. It is just a large piece of card, with the middle cut out. (Remember that the 'arch' over the 'stage' must be big enough for the puppets to appear in.) You can decorate the edges which the audience sees, for example, making it look as though there are curtains hanging at the sides. Cut strips of card for supports and position your theatre at the edge of a table (as shown on page 119). You then kneel or sit behind the table and work the puppets from below. Put a cloth on the table to hide you from the audience. Don't let the audience see your hands.

PAddingtoN.

Aunt Lucy.

Mr. Brown.

Mrs. Brown.

The Play

Paddington enters. He looks around the 'stage' and then peers at the audience.

Paddington That's strange. (He makes counting movements) One, two, three . . . four, five, six . . . seventeen, eighteen, nineteen . . . take away four . . . add ten . . . That's *very strange.* It's definitely June the twenty-fifth today. My summer birthday . . . (to audience) bears have *two* birthdays a year, you know. And yet . . . there's no-one here.
Mr. Brown enters.

Mr. Brown 'Morning Paddington.

Paddington Hello, Mr. Brown. I . . .

Mr. Brown Sorry I can't stop. I have something special to do.
Mr. Brown exits.

Paddington Oh! Oh, well, I expect he's got a lot on his mind. (darkly to audience) Trouble at the office!
Mrs. Brown enters.

Mrs. Brown Oh! Oh, there you are, Paddington. Er . . . good-bye.
Mrs. Brown exits.

Paddington	(nearly falls over backwards with surprise) *Goodbye!* Don't say Mrs. Brown's forgotten what day it is too. SONG (OFF) Sung by Mr. and Mrs. Brown and Aunt Lucy. Happy birthday to you. Happy birthday to you. Happy birthday, dear Paddington, Happy birthday to you. *Mr. and Mrs. Brown enter accompanied by Aunt Lucy.*

Aunt Lucy **Paddington** **Mr. Brown**	Paddington! Aunt Lucy! We thought you'd be surprised. She's come all the way from Lima by courtesy of the Home for Retired Bears. They had a special bazaar to raise the money for her fare.
Mrs. Brown	What do you say to that, Paddington.
Paddington	I think (pauses) I think it's the nicest birthday I very nearly didn't have, Mrs. Brown.

THE END

Make a Collection

Mr. Gruber's shop on Portobello Road is crammed full of antiques and junk. He often has people coming in to look for something they specially collect – from copper kettles to old marmalade jars! Making a collection can be great fun. It is best to have a theme, or to build your collection around one type of thing. Then if you start collecting – jugs, for example, you will probably find that friends start looking out for unusual ones to give you as Christmas or birthday presents. Here are some ideas which Mr. Gruber suggests might start you off.

Shells and pebbles
These are good to collect, and they are free! Look out for unusual shapes and colors. When

you have a fair number collected, the best way to display them is in water. Wash them, then put them in a glass bowl (an old fish bowl is ideal), and cover them with water.

Bears

Collect all sorts of bears, and display them on a shelf. Perhaps you already have an old teddy bear. Look out for wooden bears, chocolate bears, glass bears, glove puppet bears, embroidered bears, stamps with bears on, books about bears (like Rupert and Winnie-The-Pooh, as well as Paddington).

Postcards

Paddington collects postcards and sticks them in his scrapbook. You can display postcards by covering a panel of a door or cupboard with felt. Then criss-cross it with colored tape. Secure the tape where it crosses with drawing pins. Now you can arrange the postcards as shown. Look out for old postcards with embroidered silk pictures, old photograph postcards of the area you live in, funny seaside postcards, children's postcards, postcards of famous places you visit, postcards of favorite paintings (you can get these at art galleries and museums). And, of course, ask all your friends to be sure to send you postcards from their holidays.

Jigsaws

Collect old jigsaws, circular jigsaws, simple wooden jigsaws. Collect jigsaws with a theme – map jigsaws or wildlife jigsaws (showing birds or butterflies, for example). A good way to display jigsaws is to stick the finished puzzles onto board, and hang them on the wall.

Keys

Look in junk shops, and ask all your friends for old keys. Try to get as many different sizes and designs as possible. Polish up brass keys. Paint old metal keys glossy black. When you have a really big collection, hang them from little hooks set into a pegboard as shown. Arrange them in rows from the largest to the smallest, or in a pattern of your choice.

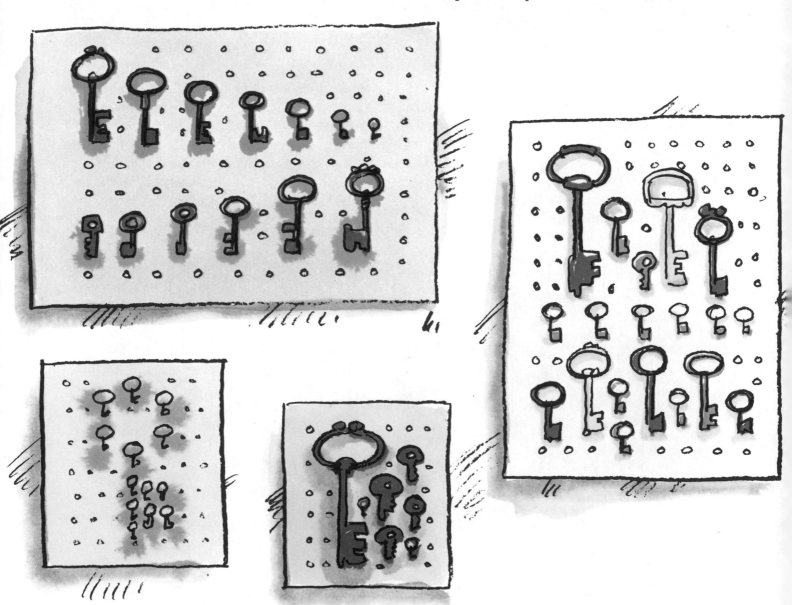

THE MARK II SHOPPING BASKET-ON-WHEELS HAS THE EXCLUSIVE SAFETY FEATURE OF INSTANT COLLAPSE ON IMPACT

WHAT A BIT OF LUCK I ALWAYS GO FOR THE OPTIONAL EXTRAS!

Party Time

Everyone loves parties, especially Paddington. Here he is to help you and your family plan a successful and happy party. There are hints and tips on how to organize a party, ideas for decorations, lots of party games and a selection of 'Paddington Tested' recipes.

There are plenty of good occasions for having a party: birthdays, or holidays like Easter or Christmas, Valentine's Day, Forth of July or Hallowe'en.

The best parties look as if they've just 'happened', but have really been carefully planned beforehand. This means lots of hard work, especially for the grown-ups, but it is worth it in the end. Then you'll enjoy your party as much as your guests!

Before the Party

Start planning a party with your parents about three weeks ahead. Decide on a date and time, and how many friends you want to invite. This depends on how much room you have, but a dozen children is probably the most you can manage. Choose friends who are about the same age.

Make a list of their names and addresses.

Write the invitations and leave about two weeks for your guests to reply.

You could buy invitation cards at your local stationers, but it's *much* more fun to make your own.

Invitations

Decorate your invitation cards to suit the occasion. Make them look as fun and as 'inviting' as you can.

Always remember to give:
- the date of the party
- the time it will begin and when it will end; three hours is a good length of time
- say who is giving the party and why; it's embarrassing wondering whether or not to bring a birthday present
- tell your guests if they should wear a costume, or special clothes
- give the address where the party is being held; if you live somewhere hard to find, enclose a small map
- put R.S.V.P. at the bottom of the invitation. This means 'please let us know if you are able to come or not'

Plans

Most parties include playing games and having food but beyond that, it's up to you. After all, it's your party!

Make out a program of events. Plan how to get your party off to an exciting start. Decide which games to play and roughly how long they will take. Don't let any one game go on for too long, and always have a few extra ones.

PLAN THE FOOD! Food should come about midway through the party. Choose from Paddington's favourite recipes.

Decide where to have your party. It's great fun to be outside in the summer, but be prepared for a rainy day, just in case.

Leave time in the morning of the party to clear the room, removing any breakable ornaments.

Set up the a table, complete with dishes, decorations and place-markers, preferably in another room.

On the Day

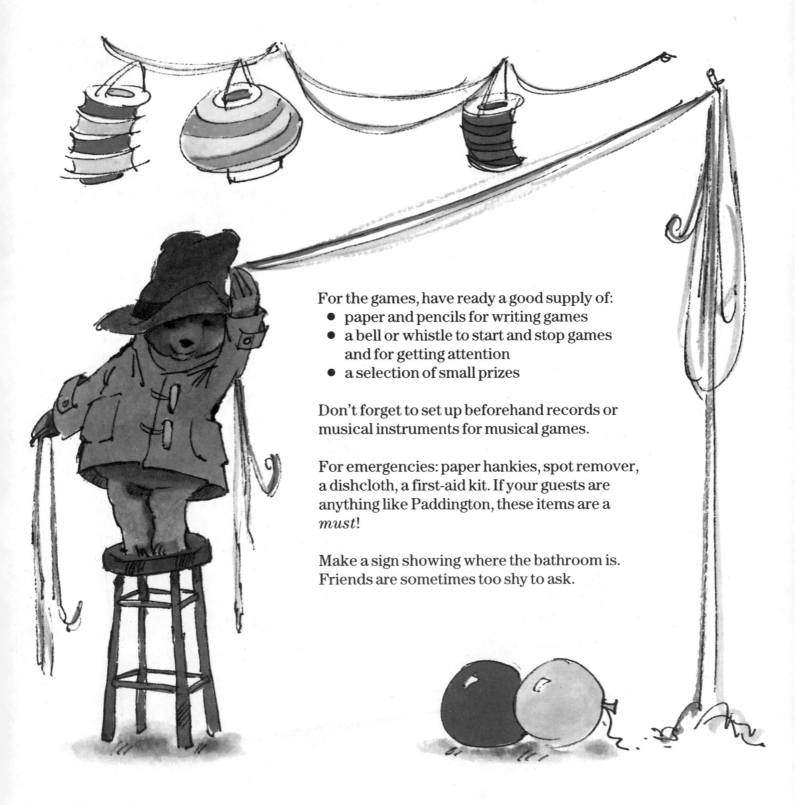

For the games, have ready a good supply of:
- paper and pencils for writing games
- a bell or whistle to start and stop games and for getting attention
- a selection of small prizes

Don't forget to set up beforehand records or musical instruments for musical games.

For emergencies: paper hankies, spot remover, a dishcloth, a first-aid kit. If your guests are anything like Paddington, these items are a *must*!

Make a sign showing where the bathroom is. Friends are sometimes too shy to ask.

Decorations

Hang colored balloons outside to welcome your friends, or pin a notice to the door saying 'Party'.

Hang up balloons, streamers, flowers, paper chains or flags. Thread candies, popcorn or fancy-shaped cookies on a string. These can be attacked at leaving time.

Pin up paper cut-outs or friezes to fit your party theme: hearts for Valentine's day, snowflakes for Christmas, black cats for Hallowe'en, skull and crossbones for a pirate party, or Wild West 'Wanted' posters for cowboys and Indians.

Decorate your tea table to match too. Fold paper napkins into pretty shapes. To show your friends where they are sitting, write each name on a cupcake or cookie with icing as a delicious place-marker.

THIS WAY

THIS WAY TO PADDINGTON'S PARTY

Party Openers

It's important to get your party off to a good start. Not all your guests may know each other, so to help break the ice, start with a game everyone can join the moment they arrive.

Try this one: Give each guest the same number of used matchsticks; six is a good number. The players take some of the matches and hide them in one clenched fist. They then challenge another guest to guess whether the number of matches held is odd or even. If the other player guesses correctly, he wins one of the matchsticks. If he's wrong, then he hands over one of his own matchsticks. After ten minutes the player with the most matchsticks is the winner.

If you plan to play team games, then it's best to choose the two teams beforehand to prevent arguments and hurt feelings.

To do this, paste two pictures cut from a magazine onto a piece of cord. Then cut each card into as many pieces as there are members on each team. Write each guest's name on the back of a piece. Give each guest their own piece when they arrive. The teams are formed by fitting the pieces together like a jigsaw puzzle; each half is in a different team.

Remember it's always a good idea to have a grown-up present while you are playing games to referee, play the music and help out.

Team Games

Passing the Bun Money

Two teams line up opposite each other, with arms outstretched and palms facing downwards. They close their eyes and the person in charge places a coin on the hand of the first player in each row. When the whistle blows, the leaders slide the coin from one hand to the other, and then onto the hand of the player next to them, and so on down the line. If the coin is dropped, it must be returned to the start, and sent on its way again. The first team to get their coin to the end of the line wins.

Blowing the Balloon

Each team forms a circle. The person in charge throws a balloon into the middle of each circle. See how long you can keep it up in the air by blowing. No hands or paws allowed!

Journey to Darkest Peru

Two teams stand in separate lines at one end of the room, facing two suitcases full of clothing. Ideally, the clothes should be things Paddington wears: a duffle-coat, floppy hat, scarf and wellington boots, but you can use other items as long as each case contains exactly the same clothing. Put a ticket labelled to DARKEST PERU in each suitcase.

On the word GO the first member of each team runs to the case, opens it and puts on all the clothes. He then runs back to his team carrying the case, takes off all the clothes, puts them back inside the case and returns the case back to its starting position. The next team member races to the case and repeats the same clothing changes. The first team to complete all the changes, return the case to its starting position, and present the person in charge with the ticket to DARKEST PERU wins the game.

Musical Games

The following games need a grown-up playing the music either on a piano or other musical instrument or on a record player.

Pass the Marmalade Sandwich

The players sit in a circle and one person is given a small parcel which looks like a marmalade sandwich. While the music plays, they have to pass the parcel to the next person on their right. As soon as the music stops, everyone freezes. The player who is holding the parcel drops out of the game, until there is only one person left.

Musical Chairs

Place some chairs in a row with every other chair facing in the opposite direction. There should be one less chair than there are players. When the music starts the players walk around the chairs. When the music stops they have to sit down on the nearest one. The unlucky player with nowhere to sit is out of the game. Another chair is removed before the next round. The player sitting in the last chair is the winner.

Musical Objects

Put a pile of different objects in the center of the floor. There should be one less object than there are players. Everyone dances round the pile, and when the music stops, each player must grab an object. The unlucky person drops out. The objects are put back in the pile, but with one less this time, and the music starts up again. The one who grabs the last object is the winner.

Paddington's Musical Hat

The players sit in a circle. One person is wearing a hat, the more like Paddington's floppy hat the better. While the music plays, the players put on, take off and pass the hat. The person wearing or holding the hat each time the music stops, is out of the game. The player left at the end is the winner.

More Games

Paddington's Postcard to Aunt Lucy

The players sit on the floor in a circle. One person is chosen as Paddington and is given a postcard which says: *I wrote a postcard to my Aunt Lucy in the Home for Retired Bears, and on the way I dropped it.* Paddington walks around the outside of the circle repeating this over and over again. At one point he drops the postcard behind one of the sitting players. The player picks up the postcard and chases Paddington around the circle. Paddington tries to sit down in the empty spot before he is caught. If he succeeds the player chasing him becomes Paddington and starts the game again. If Paddington is caught, *he* has to try again!

Mr. Curry's Footsteps

One person is chosen as Mr. Curry. The other players form a line along a wall, while he stands away from them facing in the opposite direction. The players creep up and try to touch him without being seen. Every so often Mr. Curry turns unexpectedly. If he sees anyone moving, they have to go back to the wall. The first person to touch Mr. Curry, without being caught, is the winner.

145

Gathering Wool

Before the party, take three different colors of wool and cut them into many short pieces. Hide them around the room. The players hunt for as many pieces of wool as they can find. When most of the wool has been gathered, stop the game and count the score. Each color is worth a different number of points, for example: three for red, two for blue, and one for green. Tell the players this before the game starts! The player with the highest score wins.

Mrs. Bird Says

Ask a grown-up to be Mrs Bird. Mrs Bird faces the players and gives an order, such as "Mrs Bird says, Stand on one leg" which the players must obey.

But if the words 'Mrs Bird' are left out, the players must not obey the order. If Mrs Bird catches someone moving when he shouldn't, then he must drop out of the game. Anyone who fails to obey a 'Mrs Bird' order also drops out. The one left at the end is a winner.

Mrs Bird can then announce, "It's time for a snack!"

Tea

For most children eating is the high spot of any party.

Have the table already set with dishes, decorations and place-markers.

Very small children are more comfortable with low tables, but if this is difficult to arrange, make sure there are plenty of old cushions to put on the chairs.

Using disposable paper cups, plates, forks, spoons, tablecloth and napkins saves washing-up. Drinking through straws is great fun and often avoids spills. Make sure you have plenty of extras of everything.

Some of Paddington's Favourite Recipes You Can Help to Make

After playing games your guests will be ready for a cool drink. Here's the recipe for *PADDINGTON'S PARTY FIZZ*

Squeeze the juice from an orange and half a lemon into a bowl. Cut an apple into small pieces and let them soak in this juice for a few minutes. Pour a large bottle of soda into a jug and add the fruit juice. Stir gently to avoid losing too much fizz. Chill, then serve with a dollop of ice cream in each glass.

This makes enough fizz for about six small glasses.

large bottle of Cola

INGREDIENTS

One Orange

One Apple

Ice Cream

half a lemon

Sandwiches

Sandwiches are a must for any party, but that's no reason for them to be dull. Use your imagination! Use brown and white bread to make the sandwiches more interesting; you can even make a chequer-board! Use sliced bread and cut off the crusts. Soft butter makes spreading easier. Experiment with cutting the sandwiches into unusual shapes with pastry cutters. Try making animal shapes.

Fillings

Cheese, sliced meat and jelly are great sandwich favourites, but here are some other suggestions:

Cream cheese flavoured with lemon juice is a good sandwich base. Mix it with: chopped walnuts or peanuts or cucumber; for a sweeter mixture add chopped dates or tinned peaches, apples or pineapple.

Paddington loves peanut butter best with marmalade, but you can add a layer of jelly or honey, grated apple or banana if you prefer.

Hardboiled eggs mashed up with mayonnaise and a dash of salt and pepper: add chopped ham or sardines, with or without ketchup.

Tinned salmon, tuna fish, or sardines mashed up with mayonnaise and a dash of lemon juice: add chopped tomato, cucumber or relish.

Try not to make the sandwiches too long before the party. If you have to do so, wrap them in cellophane to keep them fresh. If you are making sandwiches using fresh fruit, you must make them at the last minute or else they will discolor.

Put each kind of sandwich onto a separate plate and label it all clearly.

151

Cold Snacks

Small sausages on sticks disappear like magic. Stick them into half a grapefruit to make a hedgehog.

Potato chips with dips made from tomato sauce, cream cheese or mayonnaise mixed with chopped celery, cucumber or onions. Tuna fish mixed with sour cream is another delicious dip.

Cold cooked chicken drumsticks which children can eat with their fingers. Keep an eye open for greasy paw marks afterwards.

Jello: make three different colours of jello. When they have set, cut them up into bite-sized cubes. Serve them in individual bowls, mixing up the colors. Fruit salad or fresh berries in the summer-time, served with cream or ice cream.

Banana splits: slice a banana in half lengthwise. Place one or two scoops of ice cream on top. Put out bowls of chocolate sauce, honey, fruit syrup, chopped fruits and nuts, coconut, or chocolate chips for the guests to add themselves. Top off each banana split with whipped cream.

Anything with chocolate is a great success, but again watch the fingers!

Hot Snacks

Crackers (large ones!) sprinkled with grated cheese and grilled until the cheese melts.

Spear alternate chunks of ham and pineapple on cocktail sticks, brush with some warm corn syrup, and lightly grill.

Spread some peanut butter on small lengths of bacon. Roll up like a swiss-roll, spear them on cocktail sticks, and grill.

Any fruit — tinned peaches, pears for instance, cut into small cubes, rolled in bacon strips, speared and grilled.

Aunt Lucy's
Layer Delight

Try making this delicious dessert which is served at the Home for Retired Bears in Lima on their annual Open Day Festival.

For every two friends you will need:

a small carton of plain yoghurt
an equal quantity of cream
about 8 grapes, peeled and cut in half
2 tablespoons brown sugar
2 glacé cherries

Mix together the yoghurt and double cream

Take one tall glass with straight sides for each guest. Fill the glass with alternate layers of the cream and yoghurt mixture, the sliced grapes and brown sugar. Top with a cherry. Store in the refrigerator until serving.

Decorating the Cake

The centerpiece of any birthday party tea is the cake. But after sandwiches, snacks and other treats, no one can eat a very rich cake. To make a light and simple cake all you need is:

a Swiss Roll or two, icing and a little imagination.

Decorate your cake with candles, all kinds of candy, marzipan animals, nuts, berries, candied fruit and designs with colored icing.

Why not try making a cake shaped like Paddington's hat?

To make a hat: take a large round cake for the brim. On top of it place one or two smaller and thicker round cakes for the crown. Cover the whole hat with chocolate frosting. Make a brim of chocolate frosting around the bottom.

Write the name in white icing on top of the cake.

Games to Play After Tea

After tea it's a good idea to play quiet, sitting down games.

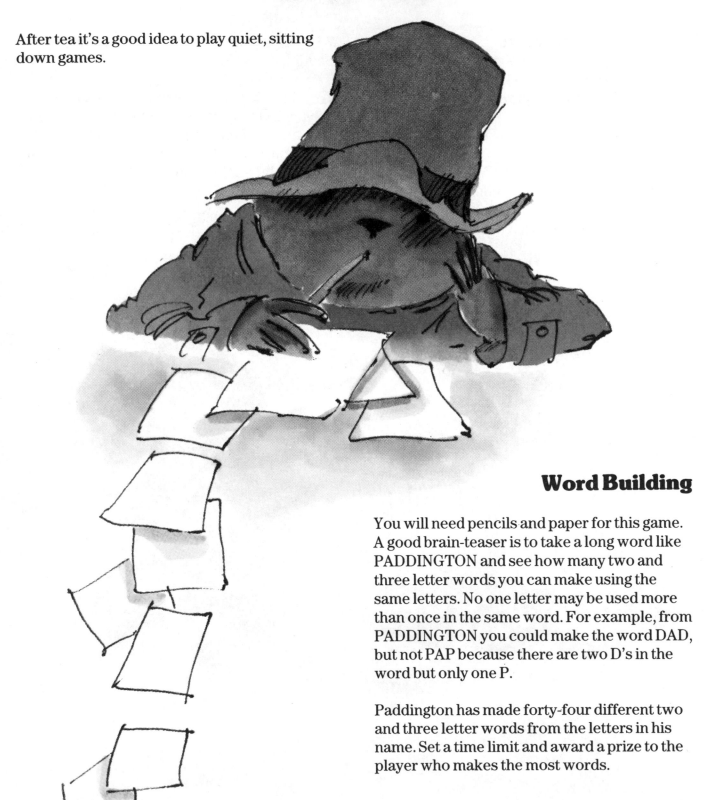

Word Building

You will need pencils and paper for this game. A good brain-teaser is to take a long word like PADDINGTON and see how many two and three letter words you can make using the same letters. No one letter may be used more than once in the same word. For example, from PADDINGTON you could make the word DAD, but not PAP because there are two D's in the word but only one P.

Paddington has made forty-four different two and three letter words from the letters in his name. Set a time limit and award a prize to the player who makes the most words.

Mrs. Bird's Tray

This game is a good test of memory. You will need pencils and paper.

A tray on which there are some ordinary objects is brought into the room. The players sit in a circle around the tray and have three minutes to memorize what objects are on it. The tray is then removed and everyone makes a list of the objects they can remember. The player with the most correct items wins.

Take a Stick

Place some cocktail sticks in a pile on a tray. Each player removes one stick in turn. If any of the other sticks move, the player is out of the game. If a player removes a stick without disturbing any of the others, then he has another turn. The game may be repeated so that everyone has a fair chance. This game really needs a grown-up to referee.

Time to Go

When the party is nearly at an end, avoid starting any new games where there is an outright winner, or no one will want to leave before it is over. While they are waiting to be collected, ask your guests to draw Paddington Bear with their eyes blindfolded. The results are bound to make the guests leave laughing!

Have a tiny present ready for each of the guests as they leave. Lucky dips from a bucket or pillowcase filled with sawdust are always fun. Wrap the presents for opening at home.

Apron

If you're even half as messy as Paddington, you should wear this everlasting apron before you try any of the activities in this book.

You will need: shelf paper, newspaper, paperclips, four pieces of ribbon, Scotchtape, pencil, scissors and a cloth apron.

Using a cloth apron as a guide, draw an apron on the shelf paper. Cut out this shape.

Cut the same apron shape out of several sheets of newspaper. Place them on top of each other. Clip all the sheets together. Scotchtape four pieces of ribbon to the inside of the apron, as shown. Wear the shelf paper side of the apron nearest to you. You can throw away the newspaper sheets as they get dirty.

Sellotape

ribbon

too big

too small

Bottle Painting

Collecting bottles is one of Paddington's favorite hobbies. They come in all sorts of fascinating shapes and look even nicer if they are decorated in bright colors.

You will need: lots of bottles – clean and with labels removed, white emulsion or matt paint, glossy colored paints and some paintbrushes. Spread newspaper over your work area.

Paint the outside of the bottle with the white paint. Let it dry. Then paint your design over the white background, or use a dark color for the background and then paint a pattern in lighter color afterwards.

Finish off by gluing an old ping-pong ball on to the neck of the bottle and painting that too.

Compass

If you ever get lost in Darkest Peru, here's how to make a compass to help you find your way!

To make a very simple compass you will need: a horseshoe magnet, a large needle, a small piece of cork, glue and a bowl of water.

Stroke the pointed end of the needle thirty or forty times over one end of the magnet. Place it lengthwise and glue it across the middle of the cork. Place the cork in the bowl, making sure the needle is above water. The needle will swing in a North to South line, and either the pointed end or the 'eye' will be facing the North Pole.

You can tell which end of the needle is facing North, if you remember that the sun rises in the East, and if you face North then East is always on your right.

Drums

Paddington saves his empty marmalade jars to make into drums. So can you.

You will need: a jar (it doesn't have to be a marmalade one), a sheet of thin, smooth paper and a rubber band.

Wet the paper and put it over the open end of the jar. Hold it in place with the rubber band. Leave it to dry. As the paper dries, it will tighten. Trim away the edges of the paper. Decorate the outside of your drum with old labels or paint. Beat your drum with pencils.

Make another drum in the same way from a larger jar or tin and notice the difference in sound.

Paddington is always careful not to play his drums too loud because it upsets Mr. Curry.

Eggshell Dragon

Whenever Mrs. Bird cooks with eggs, she saves the eggshells for Paddington. Ask your family to do the same so that you can make an eggshell dragon.

You will need: crushed eggshells, a piece of cardboard, glue, paints and a paintbrush.

Draw the outline of a dragon on a sheet of cardboard. Spread a little glue inside the outline and press on the pieces of eggshell. Allow time to dry. Then carefully paint the shells to look like a dragon.

Fingerprint People

First make an inkpad by wrapping a piece of foam rubber in an old bit of cloth, and squeezing it into a small metal container about the size of a small pipe tobacco tin. Soak the pad in *washable* ink and leave it to dry out a little before using.

You will also need: white paper, a felt pen and tissues to wipe your hands. Spread newspaper over the surface where you'll be printing.

Put your thumb or finger lightly on the inkpad and then press it firmly on to a sheet of paper. Use these fingerprints as bodies. Add arms, legs and a face with a felt pen.

Now make your own Christmas and birthday cards or design your own cartoon strips.

Growing Things

You will need: a saucer, blotting paper and seeds. Alfalfa, grass or bird seeds are all suitable.

Line the bottom of a saucer with several layers of blotting paper. Wet it and then sprinkle seeds on top. Keep the saucer in a warm place and sprinkle it with water every day. Soon the seeds will sprout.

It's even more fun to grow a potato head. Slice the bottom of a potato so that it will stand upright. Cut off the other end and scoop out a hollow in the potato. (You may need a grown-up to help you with this.) Line the hollow with blotting paper. Sow the seeds as above.

If you make a face in the side of the potato by cutting holes for mouth and eyes, you will have a potato man with green hair!

168

Hand Puppets

You can make a simple hand puppet from an old white sock. Pull the sock over your left hand, clench your fist, and draw a face with a magic marker. Or sew buttons on the face for eyes, nose and mouth. Attach some yarn to the sock with double-sided Scotchtape for hair. As you move your hand, the puppet will come alive. Make another puppet so that you can act out a play.

Make a puppet theatre by cutting the bottom out of an old shoe box and working the puppets through the opening so that your arms are hidden.

Initial Sandwiches

Paddington's special surprise treat for tea parties is an initial toasted sandwich.

Make a sandwich. In Paddington's case it's usually marmalade, but it could be cheese or anything else you like. Cut out your own or your friend's initials in kitchen foil. Ask a grown-up to toast the sandwich under the grill. When the foil is removed, the initials will show up on the sandwich in white.

Japanese Garden

You will need: a small tray with fairly steep sides or an old seed box, pebbles, paints, and a paintbrush. Spread newspaper over your work area.

The pebbles should be as round and smooth as possible – seaside pebbles are ideal. Wash them and leave to dry. Then paint them different colors. When the paint has dried, make a pattern with the pebbles in the box. Pick some flowers or make some artificial ones out of pipe cleaners and tissue paper, and 'plant' them. Japanese gardens are always simple, so use very few flowers.

Kaleidoscope

You will need: a ceiling tile or a piece of soft wood for a base, two handbag mirrors, Scotchtape, some plasticine or modelling clay, a pin, a small bead, a pencil, a cup, a piece of cardboard, paints and scissors.

Join the long sides of the two mirrors together with Scotchtape. Mount them on the base by putting a piece of plasticine or modelling clay underneath the two sides. The mirrors should be raised above the base. Make sure the mirrors are exactly as shown, with the reflecting sides facing inwards.

Push a pin into the base just inside the corner formed by the two mirrors. Slip a bead over the pin. Make sure the head of the pin sticks up above the bead.

Using a cup as a guide, draw a circle on a piece of cardboard. Cut out this circle and paint a pattern on it. When it dries, make a small hole in its center. Press this cardboard circle over the pin. Make sure it can spin freely underneath the mirror. Spin the cardboard circle and watch the changing patterns in the mirrors. Try using picture postcards in place of the cardboard.

Label Decorations

"Waste not, want not" is one of Mrs. Bird's favorite sayings. She usually saves her old labels for Paddington to decorate his jars.

Collect as many different kinds of labels as you can. They can be removed easily if the bottles are left to soak in warm soapy water for a while. Glue the labels on to a larger container, overlapping each other so that the surface underneath doesn't show. You can make a pencil holder out of a marmalade jar, decorate a wastepaper basket for your room, or decorate your drum. (See letter D).

Map Making

Paddington is very keen on maps. He was once in trouble for drawing a map of South America on the bathroom floor with Mr. Brown's shaving cream. A much less messy way of making a map is with a pencil and paper.

Draw a map of the area where you live. Show your own house and your street. Then include those of neighbors and friends, parks, your school, local shops and any other important landmarks.

When you've finished drawing the map, color it. Use dark brown for the busy main roads and a lighter brown for the smaller ones. Mark in any pedestrian crossings. Color the parks green. Label all streets and buildings.

Carry the map with you, and if you ever get lost you can show it to a policeman and ask him to help you.

Remember: the top of the map should always face North. If you don't know where North is, you can make yourself a compass. (See letter C).

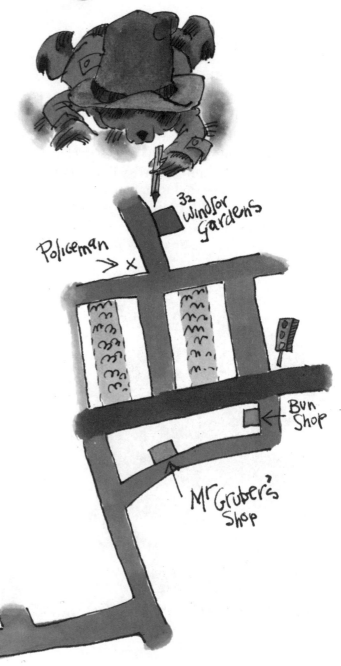

175

Necklace

Make a simple but unusual necklace from macaroni.

You will need: some thin string, paints, a paintbrush and macaroni.

Break the macaroni into pieces about half an inch long. Paint them. When they are dry, thread them onto a string. When the string is full, tie the two ends together. Your necklace is ready to wear.

Use other shapes of pasta for variety. You can also make necklaces from seeds, nuts, beans and dried fruit.

Remember to measure the string before you cut it, just to be sure that your necklace fits over your head!

Owls

To make a fat, feathery owl you will need: a round balloon, vaseline, papier mâché (see letter P), green and yellow tissue paper, modelling clay or plasticine, white cardboard, glue, paint, paintbrush and scissors. Spread newspapers all over your working area.

Blow up the balloon. Smear it lightly with vaseline. Cover all but the nozzle with four or five layers of papier mâché. Leave it to dry for a day. Tear the tissue paper into small pieces about two inches square. Glue them onto the balloon from the bottom upwards. Overlap the tissue to look like feathers. Paint two round eyes on the cardboard and cut them out. Model a beak, ears and feet with the clay or plasticine. Paint them. Glue the beak, ears, feet and eyes to the body of the owl.

Papier Mâché

Papier mâché means mashed-up paper. It's ideal for making masks, piggybanks or the owl (see letter O) because it sets rock-hard. It's messy work, so wear your apron and spread lots of newspaper around.

You will need: pieces of torn-up newspaper about two inches square and wallpaper paste. Mix the paste in a bowl and dip the newspaper scraps into the mixture. Take the pieces out and place them, one by one, over the

framework of whatever you are making. You will need as many as four or five layers. Let it dry for a day before you paint and decorate it.

Quick Clay

Here's another messy project, so wear your apron!

You can buy modelling clay, but it's more fun to make your own. Here's Paddington's own special recipe: put four measures of plain flour into a bowl. Add one measure of salt and mix together. Then add one and a half measures of water to the flour mixture. Knead the dough with your hands. At first it will be terribly sticky, but gradually it will become stiff enough to use for modelling.

It doesn't matter what sort of measure you use as long as you use the same one for all the ingredients. An eggcup makes a quantity of clay about the size of a tennis ball.

When you have made your model, put it on a baking tray. Ask a grown-up to put it in a medium hot oven (350°F – Mark 4) for you. Large, solid objects may take about an hour to bake or 'fire', smaller ones will take less time, so keep checking. Take out the model when it starts to change color. Let it cool before you paint it. Any clay left over can be stored in a plastic bag.

Robot

Have a contest with a friend to see who can make the best robot.

You will need: cardboard boxes, plastic soap containers, kitchen foil, cardboard tubes, egg cartons, string, bits of wire, feathers, spools, corks, milk bottle tops, glue, scissors, Scotchtape, paint and a paintbrush.

First make the body of your robot from a large cardboard box. Cover it with foil. Use a smaller box for the head with painted sections of an egg carton for the eyes, nose and ears. Cardboard tubes make good arms and legs. Attach dials, wires and buttons to make your robot look more authentic.

Let your imagination run wild and use all kinds of scraps and junk to decorate your robot. The stranger, the better.

Sandpaper Pictures

You will need: a sheet of fairly rough sandpaper, a sheet of stiff cardboard, glue, and scraps of colored felt and pieces of wool.

Glue the sandpaper to the cardboard. Then make pictures by pressing the wool and felt onto the sandpaper. It should stick by itself. You will find it comes away easily when you want to make a new picture.

Now tell a story, changing the pictures on your sandpaper board to fit the action.

Tank

You will need: an empty thread spool, a short but strong rubber band, two used wooden matchsticks, a drawing pin, and a small washer.

Thread the rubber band through the hole in the centre of the spool. Put a matchstick through the loop of the rubber band at one end, and pin it with the drawing pin to the spool. Thread the other end of the rubber band through the washer. Pass another matchstick through the loop on that side.

Wind up the rubber band by turning the second matchstick like a propeller. Make sure that one end of the match sticks out beyond the edge of the spool. As soon as it is fully wound, put the spool on the floor and watch it move along. You may have to practice to get it working well.

Make another tank and have a race.

Ups and Downs

U is for Up, and what goes Up must come Down. Unless it gets stuck on the way!

To make your own toy parachute you will need: an old handkerchief or square piece of cloth, four pieces of string and a weight such as a stone.

Tie a piece of string to each corner of the handkerchief. Take the four loose ends of the string and tie the weight to them. Bunch the handkerchief into a ball, throw it up into the air, and watch it float down. If the parachute falls too quickly, use a lighter weight.

An even more life-like parachute can be made from a thin piece of plastic and a figure modelled from quick clay (see letter Q). If the parachute is fairly large, use more than four lengths of string, and try making a small hole in the top. You will find it floats more evenly.

Vegetable Prints

You will need: a potato or a turnip, a knife (or help if you are too young to use one), paints and a brush or an inking pad and paper. Spread newspaper over your working area.

Cut your vegetable in half so that you have a flat surface. Draw a design on the flat surface. Cut it out. Remember that it is the raised parts of the vegetable that will show up. The parts you cut away will not print. So you'll have to think in reverse! Brush the raised part of the design with paint or ink it with a pad. Press it firmly onto the paper to make your print.

You can make your own special mark or print your initials. Paddington uses a paw print on all his letters.

Wax Scratch Pictures

You will need: colored wax crayons including black, a sheet of thick, white paper and a ballpoint pen or a knitting needle.

Color your entire piece of paper. Now cover over your drawing with black crayon until none of the colors underneath show. Using a knitting needle or a pen, gently scratch out a picture. As the black crayon is scraped away, the other colors appear as if by magic!

Whirrer

You will need: cardboard, a saucer, scissors, a pencil, paints and one metre of string.

Using a saucer as a guide, draw a circle about ten centimetres across. Cut it out. Paint a pattern on both sides and let it dry.

Make two holes in the centre of the cardboard about one inch apart. Thread the string through the holes to form a loop on one side of the cardboard. Tie the two loose ends together in a knot to make a loop on the other side.

Hold one loop in each hand. Pull on the loops, let go slightly, then pull on them again. Keep doing this until the cardboard circle spins.

Watch out! Paddington sometimes gets dizzy if he stares at his whirrer too long!

Xylophone

Make your own xylophone to play your favorite songs. You will need: some glass bottles of the same size, and a small spoon.

Stand the bottles in a row and fill them with water to different heights as shown. The more water in the bottle, the lower the note will be when you tap it with a spoon. Experiment with the water levels to get the notes you want.

On the left, stand the bottle with the most water and on your right, the one with the least. Put the rest of the bottles in order of water levels in between.

If you have five bottles, number them from one to five. Start from the left and tap out these numbers: 4 4 4 5 4 4 1 2 1 2 3 4 4.. You will be playing . . . guess what? Try it and see!

Now start playing tunes of your own. Get a friend to accompany you on some homemade drums!

Yogophone

You can make a Yogophone out of two empty yoghurt pots and a length of string.

Make a hole in the center of the bottom of each pot. Thread the string through the two holes. Tie a knot at each end inside the pot to stop the string slipping out again.

Take one phone and give the other to a friend. Walk away from each other until the string is pulled tight. Then start your secret conversations.

Zig Zag Scrapbook

Paddington always keeps a scrapbook. He fills it with used tickets, postcards, photographs, menus or anything he's collected during his many adventures. Scrapbooks are fun to make and even more fun to look back on.

To make a zigzag scrapbook you will need: lots of sheets of stiff paper and Scotchtape.

Scotchtape the pages together side by side, but be careful to keep all the pages even with each other. Fold the pages first one way and then another like an accordian. Decorate the front cover.

Start pasting!